Ruby in the Sky

Ruby
IN THE Sky

Jeanne Zulick Ferruolo

FARRAR STRAUS GIROUX · NEW YORK

Farrar Straus Giroux Books for Young Readers
An imprint of Macmillan Children's Publishing Group, LLC
175 Fifth Avenue, New York, NY 10010

Printed in the United States of America by
LSC Communications, Harrisonburg, Virginia
Designed by Elizabeth H. Clark
First edition, 2019

1   3   5   7   9   10   8   6   4   2

mackids.com

Library of Congress Cataloging-in-Publication Data

Names: Ferruolo, Jeanne Zulick, author.
Title: Ruby in the sky / Jeanne Zulick Ferruolo.
Description: First edition. | New York : Farrar Straus Giroux, 2019. |
    Summary: When Ruby Moon Hayes, twelve, and her mother move to tiny
    Fortin, Vermont, Ruby is surprised to make friends at school and in the
    neighborhood, where a reclusive lady hides a huge secret.
Identifiers: LCCN 2018008121 | ISBN 9780374309053 (hardcover)
Subjects: | CYAC: Friendship—Fiction. | Single-parent families—Fiction. |
    Moving, Household—Fiction. | Middle schools—Fiction. | Schools—Fiction. |
    Recluses—Fiction.
Classification: LCC PZ7.1.F4697 Rub 2019 | DDC [Fic]—dc23
LC record available at https://lccn.loc.gov/2018008121

Our books may be purchased in bulk for promotional, educational, or
business use. Please contact your local bookseller or the Macmillan Corporate
and Premium Sales Department at (800) 221-7945 ext. 5442 or by e-mail at
MacmillanSpecialMarkets@macmillan.com.

For my mother, Barbara Yauch Zulick,
who taught me how to be brave

Ruby in the Sky

CHAPTER

1

Sometimes people disappear. One minute they're there, then *poof,* like a magic trick, they're gone.

On that first Saturday after we moved to Fortin, Vermont, when I watched my mom get handcuffed and placed in the back of a police cruiser, that's what I thought about. People disappearing.

I'd just handed Mom the tape to seal the drafty windows of our latest "forever home" when Bob Van Doodle barked. We peered outside as the cruiser fishtailed up our unplowed driveway. Mom dropped the tape.

"He must be here about my complaint," she said. "He must have questions. Or paperwork. Remember how

Dad hated paperwork?" She pressed her necklace's moon charm against her lips.

The officer raised his hand to knock, but Mom had already opened the door. A blast of frosted air propelled him inside. The door shut. The window rattled. I hugged myself.

"Dahlia Hayes," he said.

"Yes?" Mom said.

"Ma'am, you have the right to remain silent." He handed her a piece of paper.

She glanced at it. "But this isn't right," she said in a small voice I'd only heard once before. "I was the one who made the complaint. I'm the victim. I spoke with Detective Doyle. Did you talk to her?"

"You have the right to an attorney. If you cannot afford an attorney, one will be provided to you by the court." He removed handcuffs from his belt. "I'm going to need you to come to the station for booking." His hand rested on his holster. "Put your hands behind your back."

"Booking? For what?" She crossed her arms. "You are not putting those on me."

"Simple Assault. It's all in the arrest warrant," he

said. "You're facing up to a year in jail." He jangled the handcuffs. "I prefer we not do this in front of the girl."

Mom's laugh was high-pitched and forced. "We're not going to do anything in front of *the girl*. I'm not going with you."

"Ma'am, if you make this difficult, I'll add a charge of resisting arrest. Your choice."

The officer turned toward me. I read the name tag on his uniform: OFFICER PRATTLE.

"How old are you?" he said.

I felt the lump in my throat grow, the way it always did when I had to talk to strangers. It felt like a peach pit, scratchy and tight and blocking my words from escape. I nodded my long black hair forward. My bangs were like my own personal invisibility cloak; I could disappear inside it whenever I wanted to.

"Ruby's twelve," Mom said. "And she's staying right here."

Officer Prattle took a deep breath. "Do you have something else to put on?" he asked her. She was wearing Dad's old Tim McGraw T-shirt and the sweatpants she'd slept in last night.

"Ruby, hand me my coat."

My body wouldn't move.

"Ruby," she whispered.

I grabbed her coat from the couch and held it out. She slipped her goose-bumped arms into its sleeves.

"You need to put your hands behind your back," the officer said.

Mom made tight fists and, for a second, I worried she'd slug the guy. Instead, her hands fell to her sides. The handcuffs clicked. Bob barked.

"What's your dog's name?" the officer asked me.

"Bob Van Doodle," Mom said. "My husband named him."

"Is there a neighbor who can stay with your daughter, or is she coming with us to the police station?"

Mom shook her head violently, then turned toward me, her eyes wide and unfocused. "The phone's in my bathrobe, Ruby," she said. "Call Cecy."

•———•

When they were gone, I lifted Mom's bathrobe from the chair where she'd tossed it earlier. I buried my face in it, breathing her mango-scented shampoo. I swallowed hard. *Do not cry. Do not cry. Do not cry.* Bob retrieved the tape with his teeth and dropped it at my feet. Mom's words from just before the officer showed up echoed in my brain.

This is it, Ruby, she had said. *Our true forever home. I can feel it in my bones.* She had given me a tight smile. *We hit a few bumps when we first moved to Myrtle Beach, and Avalon, and, well, Orlando, too, but everything worked out in the end.*

Only it hadn't.

Call Cecy.

Cecy had lived in Fortin her whole life. Although she was Mom's older cousin, she acted more like her mother. No matter where we had moved over the last two years, Cecy visited. *I'm your only living relative, Dahlia. I need to make sure you and Ruby are safe*, she'd say. Then she'd look at me with a face like she'd just drunk sour milk. *Your mother would have you living in a barn, Ruby, if it wasn't for me.*

Later when I'd complain about Cecy, Mom would laugh. *That's Cecy for you*, she'd say.

When things fell apart in Orlando, Cecy put her foot down. *It's time to come home to Fortin, Dahlia*, she had said. Even though Mom hadn't lived in Vermont since she was six, we packed our bags that night.

Now, as I shivered against the chill of our newest "forever home," I couldn't help but think that maybe we had finally landed in that barn Cecy was always talking about.

Bob whined and scratched at the door.

I dug Mom's TracFone out of her robe's pocket.

Cecy answered on the first ring. "I found more warm clothes at Family Thrift," she said.

I closed my eyes and breathed deeply, willing my throat to open.

"Dahlia?" Cecy said.

"It's me."

"Ruby? You sound like you just woke up. Tell your mom I'll drop off the clothes later or I can meet her at Frank's—"

"Cecy, the police were—Mom got arrested."

Silence.

"Mom said to call you."

"You've been in Fortin for less than a week. How—" Cecy swore under her breath. "And it's New Year's Day for Pete's sake. They have nothing better to do?"

I could almost see her sour-milk face.

"I'll go to the police station," she said. "I'll get to the bottom of this."

As I lowered the phone, I heard Cecy's voice screech, "Rubyyyyy!"

I put the phone to my ear.

"Stay in the house. I'll call you."

"But Bob. He'll need to—"

"Well, if you have to go out, keep him on a leash and don't go in the woods."

After I hung up, I hugged myself against the stillness of the house. Garbage bags, stuffed with whatever we could fit from our last forever home, leaned against the wobbly kitchen table and spilled off the lumpy couch. Cecy had stacked old newspapers, kindling, and logs next to a woodstove, but Mom couldn't figure out how to work it. Now it glared at me like a caged animal, its four iron legs ready to pounce.

Bob leaped up, placing his front paws on the table. He snagged his leash and dragged it clanging across the uneven floorboards toward the front door and scratched again. But I didn't want to go outside. I wanted to hide under the comforter on my air mattress.

Don't let me down, Ruby. I'm trusting you to take good care of Bob.

Bob whined.

I frowned. It couldn't be much colder outside than it

was in this freezer-box. Plus, I knew I'd go crazy sitting here waiting for Cecy to call back.

I dug through my own garbage-bag suitcase until I found a pair of jeans and Dad's old Air and Space Museum sweatshirt. I grabbed my jacket from the couch. But as soon as I stepped outside, it was clear that my Florida clothes were no match for Vermont's frozen air. It hit me like it was something solid and alive, pinching my face and making my eyes water. Each breath cut my lungs.

Bob pulled me down Specter Hill Road. Dirt and ice crunched beneath my feet. The smell of wood smoke scratched my throat. It had taken Mom and me two days to drive here from Orlando, but we might as well have traveled to the moon. I could describe Fortin in one word: gray. Gray sky, gray road, gray smells. Even Aunt Cecy with her short gray hair and glasses. Even Officer Prattle with his tight gray uniform and handcuffs.

Images of Mom getting arrested flashed through my brain. The officer pushing her head down into the back of the cruiser. The cruiser kicking up snow and dirt as it disappeared onto the road. Of course, with my dad being a cop, it wasn't like I'd never seen a police car before. Sometimes, Dad would pick me up from school in one. Sitting in its backseat, I felt safe and scared at the same time. I've always liked holing up in small spaces, like Bob Van Doodle's puppy crate. But the back of a police car is separated from the front by wire and glass and has no inside door handles. You can't get out unless someone lets you.

It must be a mistake, I thought. Mom had done a lot of weird stuff over the last couple years, but she'd never commit a crime.

I studied the dark forest on either side of me. Cecy didn't need to tell me to keep out. With each frozen gust, skeleton trees shivered their own warning: *Stay out, stay out, stay out.*

At the bottom of the hill, a rusted gate gaped open in the snow. A wooden sign hung on it. NO TRESPASS-ING, it must have once said, but now its words were faded and caked in dirt and ice. The branches of a giant pine tree reached over it like an umbrella. That's when I noticed the bunny sitting in a nest of pine needles. It was as silent as the snow itself. And still. So still, I worried it had frozen there. Only the quiver of its whiskers gave it away. Fortunately, Bob was too busy sniffing every inch of snow to notice.

I watched the bunny's fur ruffle in the breeze. Eyes wide, seeing nothing. Afraid to move, like the slightest twitch might give it away. I wanted that bunny to know she was okay with me. I longed to scoop her into my arms and bring her back to the house, where she wouldn't have to stand so still and scared by the side of the road.

Then, in a flash, the rabbit tore off. Bob ripped the leash from my frostbitten fingers and shot after her, past the NO TRESPASSING sign. I started to follow, but my sneaker stuck in the snow. After I'd hopped back to put it on, Bob was gone.

I squeezed past the gate, chasing Bob's paw prints up an unplowed driveway. Icy shivers crawled up my spine.

That's when I noticed the other set of footprints.

Then, as I turned a bend, I almost ran into a burning campfire. There was also an old farmhouse, set back, and I scanned it, searching for some sign of the person who'd built the fire. But boards covered the house's windows like bandages and snow barricaded its front door. A thick center chimney and peeling white paint made me think it was once someone's cozy home, but now it looked as tired and abandoned as the woods surrounding it.

Flames shot from the fire, licking a bright red teapot that dangled from a metal bar. A cast-iron pot steamed on a large flat rock. Nearby there was a gray shed, its front door rattling in the wind. An old quilt had been crammed inside its broken window and a shabby piece of the fabric flapped in the breeze.

"Stay out!" a sandpaper voice rasped.

I spun in dizzy confusion as the door to the shed banged open. A person dressed in a patched wool coat stepped out. A blizzard of scarves wrapped around the face so tight and thick, all I could see were two dark eyes squinting against the dim afternoon light. Every cell in my brain screamed, *Run! Go! Hide!* But my legs had frozen in place.

"Looking for something?" the voice croaked.

I scanned the woods for a sign of Bob.

"A dog shot through here. He belong to you?" It was an old lady's voice, as cracked and shaky as the shed behind her. "There are leash laws, you know. You can't let your dog run loose bothering my pets."

I blinked. I didn't see any pets. I thought about the bunny and wondered if she was okay.

The lady's eyes narrowed on me. The pit inside my throat grew. I nodded my bangs forward.

"Where'd you learn to dress?" she said. "Don't you know it's twenty-five degrees out here?"

A tiny black-and-white bird suddenly flew between us. Its flight wasn't smooth, but all crazy up and down, the way my stomach felt. I recognized the bird as a chickadee. Winter birds, my mom called them. I wished she was here. She'd know what to say to get me away from this lady.

The chickadee landed on a wire that ran from above the door of the boarded-up house, across the driveway, and then was attached to the roof of the rickety shed. Items dangled from the wire—a bright yellow coffee can, smaller tin cans, and a boot. The tiny bird took a seed and flew away.

"Who are you?" the lady asked.

I stared at my feet wishing they would move. The lady stepped closer. She smelled like black licorice. "Look at me, girl. I asked you a question."

I peeked through my bangs, feeling like the rabbit. Eyes wide, seeing nothing. I swallowed hard. My throat itched. "Ruby," I whispered.

"Where'd you come from?"

I pointed in the direction of our newest "forever home."

"Old man Specter's farm?" She squinted at me, her forehead wrinkling. "No one's lived there since he died."

I hugged myself.

The lady sniffed. "You need to keep a better handle on your dog. He can't be roaming around here."

I heard a sharp bark from behind the boarded-up house. *Bob!* I took a step toward it, then felt a tug on my hood. I turned, realizing the lady had snatched it with her claw-like hand.

"You're trying to get inside!" she hissed.

I tried to scream, but only air came out. The lady let go. I was about to run when Bob appeared, steaming and panting and grinning as if this had all been part of some fantastic game.

I grabbed his icy leash, wanting to strangle and hug him at the same time.

"You got your dog, now stay away!" the lady said as she retreated into the gray shed. The door banged shut behind her. I heard a latch click. I sure wasn't going to wait around for her to come back out. I tore out of there, Bob at my heels. As we reached Specter Hill Road, the wind picked up.

When I got to our icy driveway, all I was thinking about was getting inside and hiding under my comforter. But as I neared the house, I froze. Someone was sitting on the front porch swing, wrapped in a blanket and shivering.

Mom was back.

CHAPTER

2

Bob pulled free of my grasp and galloped toward Mom. I jammed my numb fingers into my jeans and stepped onto the porch.

Mom slowly rocked the swing as she stared into the sky. "It gets dark so early here, doesn't it?" she whispered. "Darker than anywhere else we've lived."

She scratched Bob's head as I squeezed in next to her on the seat. She adjusted her blanket to cover me. Her face looked even paler against the darkening sky. Bob got distracted by a scent in the snow and bounded off, tracking it behind the house.

"Remember when Dad used to work the overnight

shift," Mom said, "and you two played your Moon Game?"

Goose bumps ran up my arms. I did not want to talk about the Moon Game with Mom. I did not want to talk about Dad.

The Moon Game began when Dad started working nights and we hardly saw each other. Dad and I had a deal. Each night at exactly eight o'clock, no matter where we were or what we were doing, we had to find the moon.

Since we're both looking at the moon at the same time, Ruby, he'd say, *it'll be like we're sitting right next to each other.* If Dad was gone before I got home from school, he'd leave a note. *I'll see you on the moon tonight,* he'd write.

One rainy night, I cried when I couldn't find the moon. Mom rubbed my back and sang to me until I fell asleep. The next morning Dad came into my room. *The important part is the trying,* he'd said. *Just because you can't see it doesn't mean it's not there.*

Mom slowly rocked the porch swing. "I was thinking you and I could start doing that. Most of the job openings I'm finding are for the night shift."

I didn't want to hurt her feelings, but the Moon Game belonged to Dad and me.

"There's no moon in Vermont," I said. Stars had begun to pop out in the darkening night sky. But the moon seemed to have overslept.

"Just because you can't see it doesn't mean it's not there," she whispered, lifting the charm of her crescent moon necklace to her lips. Dad had given her the necklace before I was born and I couldn't remember her ever not having it on. Sometimes I'd ask her if I could wear it, but she always said no.

Mom kissed the top of my head and for a moment I felt like the old mom was back. The one who used to rub my back and sing.

"What happened, Mom? Why did that cop arrest you?"

She let the charm fall against her neck. "It's . . . it's all a mistake."

But I knew it wasn't. I knew it as much as I knew I'd hate Fortin as much as I'd hated Myrtle Beach and Avalon and Orlando. Even though those places had been vacation spots we'd visited with Dad, they weren't home. And neither was Fortin.

"Why did we have to come here, Mom? Why can't we move back to DC?"

Mom bolted upright, taking the blanket with her.

I nodded my hair forward, wishing I could snatch my words back. But it was too late. Mom's cheeks sprouted red blotches.

"Don't start that again, Ruby," she said. "You know there's no going—" The sound of tires crackling over ice and dirt interrupted her. A gray pickup ground its way up our driveway.

"Perfect." Mom pulled the blanket tight around her. "Cecy's back."

———•———•———

The engine cut and Cecy hopped from her truck wearing the same dirt-brown barn jacket she always wore. She began tugging a giant blue Rubbermaid tub from the bed of her pickup. "I could use some help here!" she called.

Mom fell back onto the porch swing and nudged me up. As I made my way toward the truck, Cecy eyed my jacket and sneakers. "I knew Dahlia hadn't properly prepared for this weather," she muttered.

Bob came racing from around back, heading toward Cecy like a speeding bullet. He leaped up, knocking her sideways. "Get down!" she yelled. "Ruby! Control your dog!"

I grabbed Bob's muddy leash and pulled him off.

"For the life of me I will not understand why you got a golden retriever, Dahlia. That dog is too big." She brushed Bob's fur from her coat. "And hairy."

I looked into Bob's smiling face. *You needed to rescue me, that's why,* he seemed to say.

Cecy lifted the tub from the truck. I tried to help, but she was in a huff now. "Just keep that dog off me!"

Mom opened the front door.

"You need to shovel and spread sand. I'll get you some," Cecy said. Inside, she dropped the container on the warped wooden floor.

Bob whined as I pushed him outside and closed the door. *Just for a minute,* I told him with my eyes. He headed off to sniff Cecy's tires.

"This is what I was able to find at Family Thrift." Cecy removed the lid. "Ruby's a size ten, right, Dahlia?"

I'm right here, I wanted to say. *And I'm a size twelve.*

"It's freezing in here," Cecy said. "All that southern living make you forget how to light a fire?" She opened the stove's cast-iron door and added kindling. "I told you. You're going to have to use this to supplement the heat. The furnace is too old to do the job alone."

"Really, Cecy, this place was the best you could find?" Mom said as she slumped onto the couch.

I dug through the bin of clothes. There were a bunch of sweaters, scarves, gloves, and heavy socks, even a pair of snow boots in my size. I slipped into a brown wool dress coat and smoothed the front with my hands. It was a little snug and kind of old-fashioned, but it was warm, and there was no duct tape holding it together. Always a good thing.

"Maybe if you didn't get arrested at your first job here, you'd be able to afford a nicer rental." She stood and brushed wood chips from her pants. "I had to beg Mr. Chatty to give you that job, Dahlia. Do you know how many people would love to work at Frank's Diner? It's a huge tourist stop in ski season."

"I was a dishwasher, Cecy. Not a rocket scientist. I'm sure I can find another job."

Cecy crossed her arms. Her mouth made a tight, straight line. "That's not the point, Dahlia."

The blanket around Mom's shoulders loosened as she

set her jaw and narrowed her eyes. "You think this was my fault?" she said.

Cecy stared back.

This was not going to end well.

"Ruby," Cecy said, her gaze never leaving my mom, "I brought a casserole and a salad. Why don't you get them from my truck?"

As I opened the door, a frozen gust rattled the windows. But as cold as it was outside, it felt like beach weather compared to the icy battle brewing inside. I slammed the door behind me.

Bob trotted over, dragging his leash through the snow. I heard Cecy's voice, scolding. "What did I tell you? You're not in a city, Dahlia. You can't be running your mouth—"

"Are you saying you believe him and not me? I did not touch that man, Cecy. Chatty knocked *me* down and I reported it to the police. He must have lied so that I'd get arrested. Well, if he thinks that's going to shut me up, then he picked the wrong girl."

I scratched Bob's head. Mom and Cecy's words made my face hot. *Cecy can get her own stupid casserole,* I thought. I grabbed the dirty end of Bob's leash and we started walking. Soon we were back at the bottom of the hill near the gate with the NO TRESPASSING sign. The bunny's pine needle nest was empty. I made a mental note to bring her some food.

I stared past the sign, seeing my own footprints from earlier. If I had thought first before chasing after Bob, I would never have gone down there. Now, with night dripping over the trees, it looked even darker and creepier. I wondered what Mom would make of the lady I'd met and realized I hadn't had a chance to tell her what had happened.

A whisper-thin strand of smoke danced above the tree line. I gripped Bob's leash tighter. If he took off again, I sure wasn't going after him.

I let Bob sniff the snow until I heard Cecy's truck start up. Fortunately, she lived in the other direction. I tugged at Bob to go back.

●————————●

Inside the house, Mom sat alone at the kitchen table, the blanket still wrapped around her shoulders. There was an unopened newspaper in front of her.

"It wasn't a mistake, was it?" I said.

Mom jumped as though she hadn't heard me come in. "Well, for your information, I didn't do anything wrong. But thank you for your vote of confidence." She opened the newspaper. "If you're going to pick up where Cecy left off, don't bother. I can find my own job."

"What happened at the police station?"

"I don't want to talk about it." She put the moon charm to her lips. "It was humiliating."

"Are you going to have to go to jail like the cop said?"

The necklace dropped. "No, no. But I have to go to court on Monday."

I leaned forward. "I want to go, too."

"No, you start school on Monday." She sighed. "Cecy will go with me."

Hearing the word *school* was enough to make my throat feel tight and itchy all over again. "What does Cecy know about court?"

Mom tilted her head. "What do you know about court?" She waved her hand in the air. "They're going to give me an attorney. A public defender. It'll get cleared up."

"What if it doesn't?"

"Sometimes you have to have a little faith." Mom

leaned over the newspaper, squinting. "It explains why no one would take my application yesterday."

"What do you mean?"

She shook her head. "This mess started at Frank's Diner on Thursday."

"Your first day of work?"

"And my last. The owner—that guy Cecy knows, Frank Chatty. Well, he shoved me."

"Why'd he do that?"

"The restaurant was really busy and he was hopping-up-and-down mad that everything was moving too slowly . . . Customers were waiting to be seated, hungry people were complaining that the food was taking too long. When folks started walking out, Chatty went ballistic, screaming and stressing everyone out even worse."

"So?"

"I was carrying out a rack of glasses and when I walked past him, I told him to cut it out."

"That's it, you said *cut it out* and he shoved you?"

The left side of Mom's mouth curled in a smile. "I might have used other words."

I rolled my eyes. "How did that make *you* get arrested?"

"You're starting to sound like Cecy, you know that?" Mom sighed. "A waitress told me that it wasn't the first time he's shoved an employee. So, I did what the rest of the ladies who work at the diner should have done years ago. I marched straight to the police station and filed a complaint against him. I know a criminal assault when I see one."

"You went to the police because of a little shove?"

Mom looked me straight in the eye. "It wasn't little, Ruby. But even if it was, no one gets to put their hands on me. Ever. Not on you, either. Understand?"

I nodded.

She lifted her pants to show bruises on her shins. "He pushed me hard enough to make me fall backward. The dishwasher rack landed on me and some of the glasses broke."

Tears filled my eyes. I blinked them back. "But why did *you* get arrested?"

"The police didn't believe me—or didn't want to." Mom straightened her pants. "Frank Chatty told them I started everything . . . that I was the one who hit him. Also he had some big-shot witness talk to the police— the mayor or someone, who says he saw the whole thing and that it happened the way Chatty said it did."

"Did you show them your legs?"

"They said they didn't need to see them. I thought it was because they believed me."

"So it's your word against his and the mayor's?"

"A couple waitresses saw what happened . . . and he's done it before. Guess he's got a short fuse." Mom waved a hand in the air. "Once I get them to come forward, this will go away."

I looked at the floor.

"I'm sorry, Ruby Moon. I know this isn't the best way to start. I'm going to—" Her words seemed to catch in her throat. She pressed her necklace against her lips.

I should have hugged her right then. I should have said, *Of course everything's going to be okay.* But I knew it wasn't. I knew that nothing would ever be right until we went home to Washington, DC, where Mom acted like a real mom and we were a real family.

I got up from my chair and opened the door to my room.

"Do you want some of Cecy's casserole? It's in the fridge," she said.

I shook my head as Bob pushed past me. I closed the door, put on my pajamas, and crawled under my comforter. Bob hopped up, almost knocking me off the air mattress. He turned around two times, then lay down.

My clock read seven fifty. I dug my hand into Bob's fur as he made his going-to-sleep grunty sounds. I stared out the window, scanning the sky for that missing moon, but the night stayed empty and black. I opened my eyes as wide as I could and let its darkness fill me.

CHAPTER

3

It was still dark Monday morning as I sleepwalked into the passenger seat of Mom's Ford Fiesta. Apparently, kids in Vermont had to get ready for school in the middle of the night. I was already late when we made the white-knuckled descent down our icy driveway.

Last week, somewhere between the Woodrow Wilson and Vince Lombardi rest stops on our journey from Florida to Fortin, something happened to Mom's Fiesta. The motor went from a quiet purr to an angry roar. Now it sounded as if we were traveling to school by rocket ship. Fortunately, the parking lot was clear of kids by the time we got there.

"You don't mind if I don't go in?" Mom yelled. "I'm late to pick up Cecy. You know how she gets."

I wanted to point out that she hadn't walked me into school once since DC, when she used to volunteer in my classroom. And I wanted to say, *Of course I mind! Mothers are supposed to come in when their kids start a new school. Mothers aren't supposed to be worried about being late for court.* Instead, I grabbed my backpack.

Mom leaned over to kiss my cheek but got mostly hair. "You'll be great," she whispered as I slipped out of the car.

Even though my backpack was practically empty, it felt like it was filled with rocks. My shoulders sagged beneath its weight. When I reached the school's entrance, I turned to wave, but Mom was already gone.

———————●————————●———————

Ever since my first day of school in Avalon, I had learned a trick. If I acted silent and invisible, people actually stopped seeing me. It worked at every school I'd been to in the last two years. When I hid inside my hair and kept my mouth shut, kids stopped trying to talk to me, secretaries forgot to check if I was in class, and teachers didn't call on me. Back at Winslow Inter-mediate, I skipped an entire week before anyone real-ized I wasn't in school. By then, we were already packed for our next forever home.

After I got buzzed in, I took a deep breath and opened the door to the main office. Inside, a student was wav-ing his arms and talking to a secretary who sat behind a tall counter.

"Bryce, we've been through this before," the secre-tary said. "A missing iguana is not an excuse for being tardy." The secretary's steel-colored bun bobbed with each sharp word. I quickly ducked behind a large green plant before she saw me.

"But it wasn't my fault," he said.

"Next time it's detention," she said. "Here's your hall pass."

The boy turned to leave. When he saw me, he opened his mouth, but at that moment a girl with dark braids and a bright orange coat entered. I motioned for her to go next. The boy left.

I felt the peach pit growing in my throat, tight and scratchy.

"Melanie, this is your third tardy this quarter," the secretary said to the girl.

I started to hug myself, but my elbow knocked the plant. It wobbled loudly.

"Excuse me, young lady. What are you doing to my philodendron?" The secretary's chin jutted up, her gray eyebrows forming an angry V. I straightened the plant before it fell.

"You're breaking it! Stop that!" She raised a hand as if she was a police officer.

Orange-coat girl snatched her pass and scurried out.

A dark-haired man wearing a green sweater-vest and a bright red tie emerged from a back office. "Mrs. Levine, can you distribute these?" Noticing me, he smiled. "Ah, you must be our new student. I'm Mr. Larkin. Welcome to Fortin Middle!" He gave a big wave before slipping into his office.

"Oh. So you must be . . ." Mrs. Levine sifted through papers. "Here it is. Ruby Moon Hayes. Sixth grade." She looked at me. "That's an unusual middle name."

I stared at my feet.

"Where are your parents?"

Secretaries were always mad when Mom didn't come in on the first day.

I shrugged.

"I'll have Mr. Larkin call them." She shook her head.

"Have a seat. Someone will come for you." She pointed at a wooden bench as she spoke into her headset.

I hugged my backpack.

A few minutes later, a skinny boy walked into the office. He had wavy, jet-black hair that needed a cut. His jeans were too big, and a tight belt made them bunch around his waist. He wore a white collared shirt like businessmen wear.

Mrs. Levine smiled at the boy. "Ahmad, Ruby is new. Can you show her to Mr. Andrews's homeroom?"

Ahmad pushed up his thick black-framed glasses with his fist. "Please." He motioned me to come with him. "We are in the same class." He spoke with an accent. As we walked down a long hallway lined with red lockers, his shiny black shoes made a *click, click* sound.

When we reached a room that said LANGUAGE ARTS, the boy opened the door. Every head turned.

I peeked through my bangs to see Mr. Andrews standing at the front. He wore wire-rimmed glasses and a ponytail that fell halfway down his back. He had a scruffy beard and a flannel shirt that hung loose over corduroys. My mom used to tease my dad for wearing corduroys. *No one wears those anymore*, she'd say.

Ahmad took his seat.

"Rumor had it we were getting a new student," Mr. Andrews said as he took two large steps toward me. His pants made a *swish, swish* sound.

He pumped my hand up and down like we were long-lost friends. I liked how his eyes crinkled at the corners as if he was smiling, even though his mouth stayed straight. I almost smiled back.

"Class, let's welcome Ruby Hayes," he said. "Ruby, please take that seat next to Dakota Eton." He pointed to an empty desk behind Ahmad and next to a girl with wavy blond hair and a sleek black athletic jacket.

I moved toward the desk. Dakota stared at me with eyes so big she looked like someone had jumped out behind her and yelled *Boo!* The girl, Melanie, who had come into the office right after me, gave a quick smile. She was still wearing her orange coat.

As I slipped into my seat, Dakota scooted her chair a few inches in the other direction as if I was invading her space. When I glanced at her, she flipped her hair back as if to say, *What? I didn't do anything.*

I was relieved Mr. Andrews didn't make me talk.

Until he did. "Ruby, tell us about yourself," he said.

I didn't have to test my throat to know that no words

were going to come out. I started to hug myself but my backpack pressed on my lap. I held my arms tight at my sides and lowered my chin, forcing shallow breaths into my lungs.

Mr. Andrews waited.

And waited.

My heart pounded in my ears, but it wasn't loud enough to block the snickering.

"Ruby, where are you from?"

Out of the corner of my eye, I saw Dakota cover her mouth with both hands. She stared at me with her big, round eyes.

My backpack made a *thud* as it fell to the floor. I wished I could climb inside.

Mr. Andrews cleared his throat. "Okay, well, welcome, Ruby. We hope you like it here." He pulled at his beard. "Now, class," he said. "What I know you've been waiting for—it's time to begin preparations for the Sixth-Grade Wax Museum!"

Everyone erupted in cheers and whoops.

Mr. Andrews adjusted his glasses and lifted a paper from his desk. "Looks like this year's Wax Museum will be held on February 14." He grinned. "Can someone explain to Ruby what the Wax Museum is?"

Arms shot up.

"Dakota?"

Dakota took a deep breath. "You pick someone important and you, y'know, read about them and learn who they were married to and what they did and how they got to be famous and then we do"—she took a deep breath—"like, a wax museum where our parents and grandparents and everyone in town comes and you pretend you are that person and you have to stand really still like a statue until the spotlight touches you and then you have to come to life as that person." Dakota inhaled, finishing with a giant smile as if this Wax Museum couldn't come soon enough.

"Thank you, Dakota. Today, we begin our research at the library media center. Mrs. Canavan has a large selection of biographies, so please don't limit your research to the Internet. By the end of class, I'd like everyone to have chosen their Wax Museum subject. You are going to live with this person for the next six weeks, so be careful in your choices." Mr. Andrews clasped his hands. "Let's gather our notebooks and head over to the library."

Kids buzzed about how they already knew who they were going to be. I slipped into the back of the line behind Ahmad. He turned to face me with a grin as goofy as Bob's.

"Let me know if you need any more help, Ruby," he said. "I was new two years ago. I know what it's like."

As the line moved, I peeked through my bangs at Ahmad's back. His shoes made their *click, click* sound.

———————————•—————————

At the entrance, a tall blond woman stood beaming. "Quiet, please. You are entering a *library*," she said.

Everyone gathered around her.

"Welcome, researchers!" Her voice was clear as a bell. "You should all be familiar with the media center but let's review. To get started, we have many biographies. You can find them in the nonfiction area"—she pointed into the stacks—"arranged in alphabetical order by the subject's last name." She pivoted in the other direction. "And I know you're all familiar with our higher-speed computers, which only six of you can use at a time. We have a variety of periodicals that can be useful . . ."

She kept talking as I scanned the room. There were lots of good places to hide.

"I am here for questions! Proceed to your research!" she finally said.

As kids fought for the computers, I slipped into the fiction section. I could see Ahmad in the next row staring at me. I didn't like how he kept acting as if he was my friend just because he brought me to homeroom.

I found one of my favorite books, *A Wrinkle in Time*. I grabbed it and made my way toward a beanbag chair in the corner. My plan was to lay low until class ended. I sank into the chair wishing it could swallow me. There was no way I'd speak in public. Hopefully, Mom and I'd be long gone before this Wax Museum happened.

"That is a fine book—however, it is a work of fiction." Mr. Andrews hovered over me. His eyes smiled even though his mouth stayed straight. "You need to find a biography."

I nodded my hair forward.

"Ruby?" His eyes crinkled at the corners.

Right then, I liked Mr. Andrews. I did. But there were times when the prickly-pit feeling made my throat so scratchy and tight that even though I *wanted* to talk, no words would come out. Times like this, I wished I could do sign language or something to let

Mr. Andrews know I was not going to be part of his Wax Museum.

I had figured out some tricks that helped. Sometimes if I didn't look at the person but focused on an object, my throat would open just enough. Right then, I stared at the image on my book's cover—Meg Murry flying toward the planet Camazotz. I wished I could join her.

"I won't be here for the Wax Museum," I whispered.

"Really?" Mr. Andrews seemed surprised, as if he couldn't imagine a student missing such an amazing opportunity. "Well, you're here now, so let's see what we can find."

I blew air out of my mouth. Great, he was one of *those* teachers. The kind who thought that, with a little extra attention, I'd suddenly discover what a wondrous thing standing on a stage humiliating myself really was. Disappearing might take a little longer with this guy.

I lifted my body out of the beanbag and followed Mr. Andrews into the stacks. In the biography section, a handful of books were scattered on the ground.

"Please be more respectful," he called after two kids who scrambled away.

I knelt down to help Mr. Andrews pick up the books.

Ahmad approached us, smiling. I stood and began leafing through the book in my hand like it was the most interesting thing in the world.

"Ahmad, who did you choose?" Mr. Andrews asked.

Ahmad pushed up his glasses with his fist. "Steve Jobs, inventor of Apple computer. He was Syrian, too."

"That's a fine choice, but you're going to need more than one source. Let's see . . ." Mr. Andrews pulled out a book. "Here's a good one. Don't forget to take notes."

"Thank you, sir."

Mr. Andrews smiled as Ahmad headed for the beanbag I'd been sitting in.

"Okay, Ruby, do you have any idea who you'd like to transform into?"

I glanced at him. I had spent so much time worrying about having to speak in front of people, I hadn't thought about getting to be someone different. That part was slightly appealing.

"What are you interested in?" he asked.

I shrugged. I was interested in riding my bike to Eastern Market with Dad on Sunday mornings. I was interested in flying kites at the Washington Monument and going to the Air and Space Museum.

I was interested in staying up late to surprise Dad with a finished section of whatever puzzle we'd been working on.

"You're wearing an Air and Space Museum sweatshirt, so you must like science," he said. "We have books on Marie Curie. Elizabeth Blackwell's here. She was the first woman physician. You could be an astronaut. Neil Armstrong, Sally Ride . . . It doesn't have to be a scientist. Let's see, there's Sonia Sotomayor, Hillary Clinton. We've got Malala Yousafzai, Michelle Obama."

A loud noise erupted by the computers. Mr. Andrews's head jerked up. "I need to leave you for a moment. Start looking through the books." He made his way toward the commotion.

I stared at the book in my hands. There was an astronaut on its cover. He was enclosed in a space suit except for a visor that allowed him to peer at the moon. I recognized him as Michael Collins. I had learned about him at a *Saturn V* exhibition.

"You're going to be a boy?" Dakota appeared next to me, snapping her gum loudly.

I looked behind me to see who she was talking to, then realized it was me.

"I'm going to be Princess Diana." She blinked her long eyelashes. "She was glamorous and tragic, like me."

I thought Dakota already looked like a princess with her wavy blond hair and sparkly makeup.

"You moved into the old Specter farmhouse last week," she said.

I nodded, thinking Dakota had wrinkled her nose when she said *Specter.*

"You're from Florida, right?" *Snap.* "But your mom's from Fortin. My mom says she remembers her from when they were in kindergarten, but then your mom moved away, but she's been back to visit because Cecy Reed is her cousin. Miss Reed's lived in Fortin, like, forever."

A girl popped up by Dakota's side. She had long brown hair that fell in the same wavy curls. She wore a sleek black athletic jersey like Dakota's. FORTIN DOWN-HILL RACING TEAM was stitched in crimson letters.

"Ellen." Dakota nudged the girl. "Ruby lives on Specter Hill." She nodded at Ellen like it meant way more than I could understand. I felt the girls' eyes on me. I tugged on the sleeve of my sweatshirt.

Ahmad walked past and gave me a quick wave. I looked at my shoes.

"You know, you shouldn't hang out with that boy, Ahmad." Dakota's eyes were large and serious. "He disappears every day during lunch. No one knows where he goes. And"—she leaned in—"he's from the Middle East, like where those terrorists came from who flew into the World Trade Center."

"Yeah," Ellen said. "He's been here for two years and still can't speak English right. I don't think he's that smart."

They both paused, staring hard at me.

Dakota tilted her head. "Do *you* speak English?" she said.

Ellen giggled.

"Girls." I was grateful for Mr. Andrews's interruption. "We are finishing up here. What did you choose?"

My eyes fell on the book in my hand.

"Astronaut Michael Collins," Mr. Andrews said. "Great, so you're going to pilot the *Columbia*, Ruby?"

I shrugged. I'd write a report, but there was no way I was speaking. Dakota and Ellen had moved into the stacks and were whispering and laughing. I thought I saw Dakota point at me.

After we checked out, I got in line with the others, keeping my eyes focused on my book's cover. Michael

Collins's confident gaze stared back. A giant moon glowed behind him. I thought about him being an astronaut and heading into space and I wondered if he had been really scared to travel to such a faraway place that was so cold and empty. A place where he'd sometimes be all alone, and wouldn't know what was going to happen next.

As the line started moving, I stared into the back of Dakota's shiny black jacket and tried to pretend I could be as brave as Michael Collins.

CHAPTER

4

Later that afternoon, Dakota and Ellen giggled their way past my seat on the bus. I knew they were laughing at me—my stringy black hair or my too-small used coat. I hugged my backpack, letting its weight press against my chest. It felt as heavy to me as the idea of having to speak at the Wax Museum.

The bus traveled around a park. A large wooden sign marked its entrance: FORTIN TOWN GREEN. It was dotted with benches and swing sets buried under snow.

After letting kids off at a bunch of small neighborhoods, the bus made its way up Specter Hill. I scanned the woods for a sign of the lady's camp, but there wasn't even a thread of smoke.

At my stop, I looked for Mom's Fiesta, but the driveway was empty. I bit my lip. Did she expect me to stay here all by myself and freeze?

As I hiked up the driveway, I saw a bigger problem. The front door was banging open and closed in the wind. In Florida, our apartment door locked automatically. In my sleep-deprived coma that morning, I must not have shut it right.

I stepped onto the front porch and poked my head inside. "Mom?" I called. No answer. I took a step. "Bob?" Nothing.

Don't let me down, Ruby. I'm trusting you to take good care of Bob.

I dropped everything and slammed the door. I ran down the driveway calling, "BOB! BOB VAN DOODLE!" I listened for the clink of dog tags but the only sound was the wind.

My sneakers skidded down Specter Hill. "Bob! Bob!" I stumbled to the pine tree and frozen gate. I stared at the NO TRESPASSING sign. That's when I heard the sound of a muffled bark.

"Bob!"

And then a dog's whine, like a cry for help. It was coming from the lady's camp. I dashed down her driveway.

Stay out! Stay out! Stay out! the trees seemed to shout. But I had to find Bob.

When I got to the burning campfire, I didn't see Bob, but I could hear him. He was barking and whining from inside that crooked gray shed.

I spun, searching for the lady, but there was only the boarded-up house staring at me with its bandaged eyes. *Stay out! Stay out! Stay out!*

My heart pounded in my ears. Every ounce of me wanted to get away from that creepy place. Bob whined and a clatter like falling tin cans came from inside the shed. I could hear Bob's nails clawing the door.

I scanned the woods for the lady. Nothing.

Another sharp bark. I worried he was hurt. I inched closer to the shed and flicked the latch open. Bob bounded out, knocking me down.

"Bob! Are you okay?" Relief flooded over me until I realized I had forgotten his leash. I grabbed him by the collar. "Come on, let's get out of here." I started down the driveway dragging him, but he twisted and pulled out of my grasp. I fell backward. Snow soaked through my jeans.

"Bob! Come!" I yelled.

Bob danced around me like we were playing a game. I got up and grabbed for his collar again, but he stayed out of my reach. Tears welled in my eyes. *Do not cry*, I told myself. *Do not cry.*

"How about a thank-you?" a scratchy voice called.

I spun around to see the lady. She was still wrapped in scarves, but they were looser, revealing a wrinkled brown face. A few strands of wiry gray hair had escaped and were whipping around in the wind.

When she spoke, I saw she was missing her two front teeth. "He could have been hurt, you know. Hunters leave traps by the pond."

Bob had found a stick too large to carry, but that didn't stop him from dragging it toward her.

"I spring them every time I find a new one," she said. "So they can't catch my pets. But sometimes I miss one."

A large blue-and-white bird swooped above our heads and landed on a dangling tin can, making it spin and tip. Two chickadees flew off. More blue birds came, squawking and fighting and knocking the cans together. In their commotion, seeds spilled.

The lady ran beneath the feeders waving her arms. "Accck! Go! Go away!" she screeched. Bob joined in, running and barking. The birds flew into the forest. "Blue jays!" She cackled. "They're bullies, they are."

I swallowed hard.

"At least you have a real coat today. Now you need some good boots and a warm hat." The lady stared at me as if she was trying to look inside my brain.

I felt my insides freeze. I nodded my hair forward, but I was curious, too. Did she live in that shed?

"You must be about twelve."

I gave a quick nod.

"Twelve, twelve," she whispered as her gaze fell to her feet.

I thought about the look Dakota gave Ellen when she mentioned Specter Hill. I wondered if they thought I was as weird as this lady because I lived near her.

"Now you can return the favor." She spun on her heel and walked toward the boarded-up house. "I need you to feed my pets. The seeds are right here."

Bob leaped up and trotted after her. I thought about making a break for it, but I knew he'd never follow.

She stood in front of a giant steel garbage can that rested against the house. "My name is Abigail, by the way. Abigail Jacobs."

Bob licked Abigail's leathery hand. I rolled my eyes. *Traitor.*

Abigail absently reached down and stroked his head. Her crooked fingers reminded me of the branches on the skeleton trees. "The dog and I have come to an understanding," she said. "He's not going to bother my pets and I'm not going to shoot him." She coughed out a crazy laugh and glanced sideways at me. "You don't talk much, do you? That's good. Most people talk too much."

She lifted the top from the steel can, reached inside, and removed a wooden scoop spilling with seeds. "Black-oil sunflower seeds. Only the best for my pets," she said. "Follow me." She moved beneath the wire. "My arthritis won't let me reach like I used to."

I stared at the dangling tin cans and empty boot.

"You're going to fill these feeders, but first I need to call them over." Abigail poured the seeds into her bare hands, letting the scoop fall to the ground.

Holding her seed-filled hands in front of her, she sang out, *"Chick-a-dee-dee-dee, chick-a-dee-dee-dee-dee."*

Tiny black-and-white birds gathered in the snow-trimmed bushes. One flew toward her in its roller-coaster way. I almost fell over when it landed on her fingertips and snagged a seed. I gasped and the bird flew off. I covered my mouth with both hands.

More chickadees came, then, one at a time. Each clung to her fingertips before flying away with a seed. After a few moments, Abigail dropped the remaining seeds into the snow. "Something for the squirrels," she said.

"How'd you do that?" I whispered.

As she turned toward me, I was surprised to see that her eyes had become as blue as a summer sky.

"Magic," she said. She dug the scoop out of the snow and headed back toward the seed can. She filled the scoop and handed it to me.

My feet were so cold now, I couldn't feel my toes. I reached for a Chock full o'Nuts can. Half the seeds spilled.

"Pull on the line," she said. "It'll hold."

I emptied the scoop and handed it to her. She reminded me of the homeless people I used to see in Washington, DC. There was a man who used to sit at the top of the Dupont Circle escalator. Even in the middle of summer, he dressed in a long-sleeved army uniform. This lady reminded me of him, scary, but fragile, too. Whenever we saw him, Dad saluted and said, "Thank you for your service."

Abigail handed me another scoop. I flinched at her closeness. She still smelled like black licorice, but other things, too. Pine needles and wood smoke and winter. When our hands touched, it was like her sadness wrapped around me, as thick as the scarves she hid beneath.

As I filled the last can, Abigail moved toward the edge of the woods. From the corner of my eye I saw her drag a wooden sled filled with logs. I emptied the last of the seeds. As she came near, I grabbed the rope to help pull.

"Right here," she said, when we were in front of the shed. I handed her the scoop. As she shuffled back to the can to put it away, I couldn't help but stare at the boarded-up house.

She closed the lid and turned toward me. I quickly looked away, but it was too late, she had caught me staring.

"Stay away from there," she snapped. "There are only ghosts in that house." With that, she pivoted on one foot and shuffled into her crooked shed. The door slammed shut behind her. I heard the inside latch click into place. The only other sound was the rustling of chickadee wings.

Bob lifted his head as if to say, *Hey, where'd she go?* I turned toward the house as if it could tell me why she had disappeared, but it only stared back with its bandaged window-eyes.

Stay out! it warned.

"Bob," I said, hearing my voice crack. "Let's get out of here." This time Bob followed. We ran up Specter Hill as fast as our frozen feet would take us.

●——————●

Mom's Fiesta was in the driveway when I got back. Smoke poured from the chimney, so I knew Cecy must have stopped by. I was glad I had missed her.

"Mom," I called into the house. Bob pushed past me. I took off my coat and headed toward the sink. I drank straight from the faucet. The water was cool and clear. I filled Bob's bowl. He lapped the water as if we'd just crossed the Sahara.

Mom stepped out of her room wrapped in a blanket

over her sweats, her forehead creased with concern. "Where have you been?" she asked.

I shrugged.

She slid onto a chair at the table. "I've been waiting for you for over an hour." She pulled the blanket tight. "What were you doing?"

"Walking Bob."

"You left your backpack on the front porch, Ruby. What was I supposed to think?" She followed me with her eyes. "And you weren't just walking Bob for a whole hour. Where did you go?"

"There's a lady that lives at the bottom of the hill. She wanted me to help her."

I opened the fridge and removed Cecy's casserole.

"You didn't, did you? I heard she's not well," Mom said. "I don't want you down there."

"Why?"

"Why? Doesn't she live outside? Something's definitely not right there. What if she does something weird?"

You mean like get arrested? I thought. "You don't know her, Mom. She couldn't hurt a flea. I think I weigh more than she does."

Mom frowned. "Don't go down there. End of conversation."

The hair on the back of my neck bristled. Why should I listen? It wasn't like Mom listened to me anymore. I turned the oven on. "What happened in court? Did they drop the charges?" I asked.

"Nope." Mom pressed the moon charm to her lips. "Turns out Frank's Diner is what they affectionately refer to around here as the Mayor's Satellite Office."

"What does that mean?"

"The owner, Frank Chatty, who shoved me . . . well, he's lived in Fortin his whole life and so has the police chief, and they're all best friends with the mayor, who says he saw everything."

"So?"

"So, when it comes down to who's to blame here, who do you think the police chief picked? His old pal from T-ball days or the new girl in town?"

"You're from here."

"I haven't lived here for over thirty years." She spread her hands wide. "Welcome to Fortin, Ruby. Don't you get it? They can do whatever they want."

None of this made sense. "But what about the

waitresses who were there? Won't they say what they saw happened?"

"It's a small town, Ruby, and they're scared of Chatty." She crossed her arms. "No one wants to lose their job."

As I put the casserole in the oven, I tried to gulp back the panic that was rising in my throat. "They can't put you in jail for this, right?"

"Annie worked out a deal with the prosecutor. If I plead guilty to a lower charge like disorderly conduct, he'll give me probation and I'll only have to do some community service."

"Who's Annie?"

"My public defender. She's not like any lawyer I've ever met." Mom glanced at me sideways. "But she's tough as nails. She's the only person who's actually listened to me."

Relief washed over me. "Well, as long as you don't have to go to jail."

Mom frowned.

"What?"

"I don't want it," she said.

"What do you mean, you don't want it?"

She shrugged. "I didn't do anything wrong. I'm not going to plead guilty, even if all I have to do is community service."

"But you won't go to jail."

Mom picked at a thread on the blanket.

"What does Cecy say?" I asked.

Mom snorted. "What do you think Cecy says? She wants me to get this over with."

I removed the casserole from the oven and sliced two pieces onto paper plates. It had noodles and cream and what looked like ham and peas in it. I handed Mom a plate and sat across from her.

"None of this would have happened if we'd never come here," I said. "I know you hate it here, too." I took a bite. The casserole was still cold, but I didn't think it would taste much better hot.

"Maybe you're right." Mom moved a pea around her plate. "We haven't even unpacked yet. And things sure aren't going the way I thought they would." She put her fork down. "But I thought that this could be it, Ruby. Even though I left Fortin when I was little, I still have good memories of growing up here." She stared out the window. "You know, I used to help my dad collect sap to boil into maple syrup." She smiled. "And Vermont in the summer . . . it's so green and the air, well, you've never smelled anything so delicious . . ."

I crossed my arms.

Mom blinked. "I'd hoped that by coming back I could make some new memories with you, Ruby." She sighed. "Of course Cecy's been after me to move here ever since . . . well, I know she can be a pain but . . ." She half-smiled. "That's Cecy for you."

I rolled my eyes.

Mom's face got serious. "She's the only family we have left, Ruby. I can't do it alone."

"You're not alone, Mom. I'm here." I hated the whine that was creeping into my voice. "Aren't I enough?"

"You're more than enough, Ruby Moon. Maybe you're right. Maybe Fortin isn't our forever home. But—"

"But nothing, Mom. We need to get out of here. Let's go back to DC. Let's go back to where we were a family."

"Oh, Ruby." Mom put her hand on mine. "It will never be the same. You know—"

I jumped back as if stung. "You *don't* know, Mom. If we moved there and—"

"Ruby." Mom's voice was getting that exhausted sound that seemed to consume her lately. "Washington, DC, is over. We are never moving back there. Can't you understand? All these fresh starts . . . I'm doing this for you."

"You're not doing anything for me." My voice quivered. "You're doing whatever you want, like always. I never get a say in what we do or where we go." I shut my eyes tight. *I will not cry. I will not cry.*

"Oh, Ruby. I'm sorry." Tears wobbled down Mom's face. "I didn't mean to—" She reached out to hug me, but I moved away. She ended up hugging herself. "It's okay. It's been a long day. We should both go to bed."

Her blanket dragged behind her as she disappeared into her room.

I stared at the empty table and our uneaten dinner. Bob stretched, then turned toward me as if to say, *Well, if you're not eating that . . .*

I lowered my plate to let Bob lick it clean. At least someone enjoyed Cecy's casserole. I hitched Bob's leash and slipped into my coat. I wrapped a scarf across my face and stepped into my boots. Bob's tail whacked everything in sight. Before we left, I opened the fridge and found Cecy's salad. I shoved a handful of lettuce into my pocket. Mom had left a flashlight near the woodstove. I grabbed that and a pair of gloves, too.

Bob and I hiked down Specter Hill Road until we reached the pine tree and the NO TRESPASSING sign. I dumped the lettuce and whispered, "Come, little bunny."

The woods were thick with night and the smoke from the lady's campfire danced above the tree line. *What did she say her name was? Abigail. Abigail Jacobs.* I wondered if she was still outside by the fire or inside her crooked shed. I wondered if she was cold, too.

I scanned the horizon until I found the skinniest of moon slivers. "I'll see you on the moon tonight," I whispered. I hoped Dad could see it, too.

Standing beneath that skinny moon, I made a wish. I wished I could turn back time. I wished we were still in DC and everything was the way it was before fathers didn't come home and mothers got arrested. I thought about Mom's face as she told me about court. I'd never get her to move to DC now until her case was done, but I could do my best to speed things up. *As soon as we get court behind us*, I thought, *then we can get back to where we were before everything fell apart.*

When I couldn't stand the cold any longer, I ran up Specter Hill Road, Bob at my heels.

Inside the house, the fire had died. Bob shook off the snow and followed me into my fake bedroom. I put on my pajamas and crawled under the comforter. Bob snuggled close. Together we fell asleep, staring at that barely-a-sliver of moon.

CHAPTER

5

The next morning, as the bus made its way around the town green, I was doing my best to stay invisible when someone shouted, "Hey, look!" Kids sat up, pushing against the windows.

Like an ink blot on a blank page, a figure stood by a bench on the edge of the park. She wore a patched wool coat and was wrapped in so many scarves you couldn't see her face. Her hands stretched out in front of her as birds gathered. Abigail was feeding her pets.

"Look, you guys! It's the Bird Lady!" Dakota said.

Bryce, the kid with the missing iguana, said, "I've never seen her this close."

"I have." Dakota raised her eyebrows. "Inside her camp."

"No way," Bryce said. "No one goes down there." He held his hands like claws and made a *bwah-ha-ha* sound. "No one who's ever lived to tell about it, anyway."

Someone threw a crumpled piece of paper at him. He batted it away with his claw hand.

"I heard her house is boarded up," Melanie said. I watched her eyes dart between Dakota and Ellen as she fidgeted with the zipper of her orange coat.

"She doesn't live in her house," Dakota said.

"Where does she live?" Melanie asked.

I couldn't take my eyes off Abigail as chickadees landed on her fingertips, one at a time.

Dakota stared out the window. "She lives in a dirty shed. She won't go inside her house."

"Why not?" a boy asked.

"Really, you guys don't know what she did?" Dakota said.

Kids were still batting the crumpled paper in the air.

"Cut it out," the bus driver yelled.

Bryce slid low in his seat.

"Her real name is Abigail Jacobs. She used to live in that house with her husband and little girl," Dakota said. "But my mom says she was always weird. Like she never talked to anyone in town and was never home. One day she called the police to say her husband and daughter disappeared. The police couldn't figure out what happened for a long time. Then they found them"—Dakota glanced around—"dead!"

Kids turned away from the windows to stare at Dakota. She seemed to enjoy her growing audience.

"People knew she murdered them," she continued. "But the cops could never pin it on her." Dakota narrowed her eyes. "My mom says she knows she did it because, right after it happened, the Bird Lady became a drunk and lost her job and stuff." Dakota nodded. "It's her conscience that keeps her outside."

I thought about what Abigail had said. *There are only ghosts in that house.*

Bryce popped up. "When we go camping, my uncle always tells a story about the Bird Lady killing her family and then disappearing." He shook his head. "I can never sleep when he tells that story."

"I heard she's, like, a real witch. She always has a fire going, and she has one of those witch's pots where she mixes spells," someone said.

"It's called a cauldron," Dakota said.

We were past the town green. Kids settled back into their seats.

Dakota seems to know everything about everybody, I thought. My heart beat hard and fast in my ears. What if she found out about my mom getting arrested? My palms felt damp inside my gloves.

"You live next to her, right, Ruby?" Dakota leaned over my seat.

For a moment, I thought she meant my mom. Then I realized she meant Abigail. I wondered if she'd seen me walking Bob down there. I let my bangs fall forward.

Dakota laughed. "Ruby, have you been visiting her shed?" She sniffed the air. "I think you even smell like the Bird Lady."

I cautiously sniffed my sleeve. All I smelled was a smoky wood smell.

Ellen and Dakota started to make sniffing noises near me and then Dakota said, "Yup, definitely bird poop." The two fell into a fit of giggles.

I leaned against the window. The cold glass felt good against my hot cheek. The bus drove through the center of town, past the Babcock Library, the post office, and Rucki's Market. More kids got on. I felt someone sit on the edge of my seat.

"Hello, Ruby."

It was Ahmad. I kept my gaze focused out the window.

"I have decided that I will be astronaut Neil Armstrong for the Wax Museum," he said. "I know you are Michael Collins. We can work as a team."

Mr. Andrews hadn't said anything about partners.

"Everyone in town goes to this Wax Museum. It is very fun like a great celebration," Ahmad said. "My uncle posted an advertisement in Rucki's window."

Fortunately, the bus pulled into school. I stood and heaved my backpack onto my shoulder. Its weight pulled down on me. Ahmad stepped aside to let me go first. I pushed past him to join the kids streaming off the bus. He got stuck a few people behind me.

* ● ———————————— ● *

After fighting with my locker for ten minutes, I hustled toward Language Arts, worried I'd be late. I slid into my seat, glancing at Dakota. All of her clothes were so shiny. I looked down at my gray sweatshirt. I felt like I was doomed to be stuck in her shadow—same stupid bus, same stupid homeroom, same stupid Wax Museum.

Mr. Andrews stood at the front, his mouth serious, his eyes laughing. He reminded me of someone who knew the answer to a puzzle no one else could figure out.

"Okay, friends, settle down." He pulled at his beard.

When everyone had taken their seats, he clasped his hands. "Today we are going to talk about primary and secondary sources. If your book is not an autobiography, it is not a primary source. You are reading someone else's view, which is never going to be as accurate as your subject's own words. So how can we find primary sources?"

Hands went up.

"Sophia?"

"We can search online to find letters or books our character has written."

"Excellent. Does anyone have any other ideas?"

"If our character is alive, we can write them a letter," Ahmad said.

"Great idea. They might not write back. But why not give it a shot?" Mr. Andrews said. "So, today, that is what we are going to do. Everyone should get a laptop from the cart and begin researching primary sources."

I waited in line, grabbing the last laptop. I brought

it to my seat and stared out the window. The gray sky promised snow. I thought about Abigail Jacobs, always outside, always cold.

I opened the laptop and signed on. Mr. Andrews strolled up and down aisles helping students. I typed *Michael Collins*. Several websites popped up. I clicked on one and began jotting notes.

Michael Collins was sometimes called "the forgotten astronaut" because he stayed inside the command module *Columbia* and traveled alone to the far side of the moon while Neil Armstrong and Buzz Aldrin landed in the *Eagle*. He lived with his wife, Patricia, and their three kids. He had a German shepherd that he named Dubhe, after one of the stars in the Big Dipper, and a rabbit named Snowball. Michael Collins orbited the moon twenty-seven times during the Apollo 11 mission. Each time his spacecraft drifted behind the moon, he lost all radio contact with Earth. But Collins says he never felt lonely because he had an important job to do—he knew Neil Armstrong and Buzz Aldrin couldn't get home without him.

I tried to stay focused on Michael Collins, but the stuff the kids had said about Abigail was bouncing around in my brain. Their chatter reminded me of the blue jays I'd seen fighting and squawking at Abigail's tin can feeders.

The laptop's screensaver faded to black and in my mind's eye I could see the image of Abigail feeding the birds at the town green. She was strange enough, but could she have really killed a person? Could she have killed her own daughter?

I clicked the screen awake, and in the search field I backspaced over *Michael Collins* and typed *Abigail Jacobs, Fortin, Vermont.*

The *Fortin Citizen* archives popped up with an article headlined ABIGAIL JACOBS, 18 SPECTER HILL ROAD, ARRESTED.

"Excuse me, Ruby." Mr. Andrews read over my shoulder. "Who is Abigail Jacobs?"

I jumped at his voice.

"I thought you were doing Michael Collins?"

I exited the page. "I—I won't be here for the Wax Museum."

"Where will you be?"

I stared hard into the screen. Kids began whispering.

"Washington, DC," I whispered.

"Hmm." Mr. Andrews pulled at his beard. "Well,

until that happens, you need to keep preparing. So are you Michael Collins or this Abigail Jacobs?"

I heard Dakota whisper something to Ellen. Ellen laughed.

I felt my body shrink. "Michael Collins," I said.

"Okay, so let's get back to that." Mr. Andrews moved on.

Suddenly, I felt like I was in a shadow. I turned to see Dakota hovering over me. I stared after Mr. Andrews, but he was helping someone else.

Dakota flipped her hair and leaned in, trying to see my screen. The smell of her grape bubble gum turned my stomach.

"So you're going to be the Bird Lady for the Wax Museum?" she said. "Are you going to sleep in an old milk shed to get ready for your big debut?"

Ellen tried to suppress her laugh. It came out as a snort.

I stared at my hands.

Ahmad turned around in his seat. "Ruby is Michael Collins for the Wax Museum."

Dakota's giant round eyes felt like they were boring into my skin. "No, I think you really are the Bird Lady."

She blinked. "You don't talk to anyone. You wear the same dirty sweatshirt every day." She put her hands on her hips. "And I happen to know that your mother—"

My head whipped around, but before Dakota said another word, Mr. Andrews was at my desk again. "Everything okay here?" he asked.

Dakota flopped into her seat and began typing hard on her laptop.

"Ruby?" he said.

I nodded. "Y-yes." I typed in Michael Collins's name and a series of articles popped up. I clicked on one and began reading.

Mr. Andrews moved on.

Beep! My screen showed one new message. I clicked on it.

It was Ahmad. *I invite you to sit with me at lunch.*

Yesterday, I had ducked into a bathroom stall to eat my sandwich. It was gross, but I was hungry and the noise of the cafeteria had made my stomach hurt.

I typed back: *You're going to get in trouble for sending a message.*

We can work together on the Wax Museum.

I'm not doing the Wax Museum.

I will help you.

I don't need your help.

"Make sure you're taking notes, people," Mr. Andrews said. "You can read all the information you want, but if you aren't recording the important parts, you're going to have a hard time writing out the index cards you'll need for your presentations."

After what seemed like forever, Mr. Andrews said, "Please return your laptops to the cart. Tomorrow we will start outlining speeches." Chairs scraped as kids grabbed backpacks and made their way out of the classroom.

Ahmad turned toward me. He was wearing a black vest over the same collared shirt. He pushed his glasses up with his fist. "We have Science with Mrs. Connelly now," he said.

I didn't look up.

"You would like to sit with me at lunch today?"

I shook my head no.

Ahmad's cheeks tinged pink. He returned his laptop and scurried out. He never seemed to hang out with anyone, either.

I stared into my laptop screen. The image showed Michael Collins tucked inside the *Columbia*, staring out at the bright full moon. As I clicked *Shut Down*, the image faded and I couldn't help but wonder how Michael Collins had felt—seeing the moon so close, but knowing he would never, ever reach it.

●────────●

That afternoon, when I got back to the house, there was a note.

RUBY!!

Great news! I got a job at Rucki's Market—the one near your school (next to the post office and library). Come visit me! It's only a fifteen-minute walk from home and they serve food. I'll be there until six!

XOXO,
Mom

P.S. See, I told you things would work out!

I crumpled the note and threw it in the garbage. Maybe things were working out for her, but they weren't for me.

Bob dropped his leash at my feet. When I tried to pick it up he snatched it away again, hopping just out of my reach.

"If you want me to take you outside, drop it."

Bob danced around me, the leash still in his mouth.

"Give it, Bob."

Bob scrambled toward the door and scratched.

I fished through the bin for a hat and gloves. If I was going for a walk, it wasn't going to be back toward school.

I grabbed lettuce from the fridge. As I opened the front door to go out, Bob bolted past me. I waited with my arms crossed. Eventually he came back. I hitched the leash to his collar and we set off down Specter Hill Road.

Bob trotted in front of me, his head held high as if all his senses were on alert. The sky had cleared but the temperature had dropped. The frozen air pinched any skin I'd left exposed. The ice-covered snow sparkled in the afternoon sun. I breathed in the cold, clear air. My quick steps seemed to warm me from inside. The hat and gloves helped, too.

At the bottom of Abigail's driveway, the bunny

sat beneath her pine tree, still as a statue. I crept closer, but when I was near enough to touch her, the bunny hopped a few feet away. I held Bob's leash firmly and emptied the greens into the snow and stepped back.

As I pulled on Bob to leave, I heard a voice.

"You came back."

My stomach tightened. I turned to stare at Abigail. She seemed so tiny and delicate that a strong wind could knock her over. She smiled, revealing the gap in her front teeth.

I tried to match Dakota's story against this lady's quiet manner, but it didn't fit. Mom's words echoed in my brain: *Sometimes you have to have a little faith.* If Mom saw Abigail with the chickadees, I knew she'd want me to help her.

"You can let Bob off the leash. He'll behave."

"He'll chase the bunny."

"Give it a try."

I unhooked Bob. He took a step toward the rabbit. His body quivered.

"Bob!" Abigail snapped her fingers, and just like that, Bob trotted next to her. When she scratched the top of his head, her eyes crinkled at the corners, reminding me of Mr. Andrews. She fed Bob a treat. "I told you," she said. "Bob and I have come to an understanding."

"He never listens to me," I said.

"If you want him to listen, you have to speak up," she said. "It works on people, too, you know."

I wanted to ask her about what Dakota had said. I wanted to know why she didn't go inside her house. But somehow, I knew if I did, she'd disappear on me again. Right then, I did not want to be alone.

Abigail stared at me as if she was trying to figure something out. "You're not like them, are you?" she whispered.

Like who? I wanted to ask.

Her voice was so soft and sad that if, at that very moment, the wind hadn't died down, and the trees hadn't stood still, I might not have heard what she said next: "You're like my Lillian."

Maybe it was that she didn't make me talk. Maybe it was because I wanted to see those magic chickadees again. Maybe it was because, for some crazy reason, I liked this lady and her quiet way, but when she said, "Will you please help me feed my pets?" I nodded and followed.

As we neared her campfire, the steaming red teapot whistled. "Would you like some pine needle tea?" she asked. "It's chock-full of vitamin C."

I shook my head.

The quilt was still shoved in the shed's broken window. Its fabric must have been pink once, but now its princess pattern had turned a patchy beige.

The blue jays' commotion at the feeders reminded me that I had a job. I trudged beneath them. The blue jays took off.

I turned to find Abigail staring at me. "I think it's your turn," she said.

"My turn to what?"

"To feed the chickadees, of course." She retrieved a scoop filled with seeds. "Drop your gloves. They get in the way." As my gloves fell to the ground, cold air stung my fingertips in sharp pinpricks.

"Now stretch out your hands. Higher."

She dumped frozen seeds into my outstretched hands. Dusty pieces floated into my nose, making me sneeze. She moved near the seed can, Bob by her side.

"Stand up straight," she said. "Shoulders back, that's it, tall like a forest tree."

I felt myself grow. I glanced at Abigail to make sure I was doing it right. She motioned for me to look straight ahead. The cold air seemed to blow right through my jeans, but I forgot about that when I saw the tiny, black-capped birds gathering on trees and shrubs. Suddenly, one made its roller-coaster flight toward me.

For a split second, the bird hovered in front of me. The air from its wings brushed my cheek. I had never been that close to something so wild, and the magic of it took my breath away. The bird's claws gently gripped my fingertips and I bit my lip. The tiny bird seemed to check me out, then it claimed a seed. My head felt light and I realized I'd been holding my breath the whole time. I gasped for air and the bird flew away, a single seed clenched in its tiny beak.

Seeds spilled from my hands onto the ground. I was worried Abigail would be upset, but her face had broken into a gap-toothed grin.

"Something for the squirrels," she said.

"How did you get them to do that?" I said.

"I didn't. You did."

"But I didn't do anything."

"You did everything."

"All I did was stand here."

"You stood tall. You didn't run away. Sometimes that's enough." She stared out into the sky. I followed her gaze, finding the rising moon.

"Waxing crescent," she said.

"What?"

"The moon. It's getting bigger every day until it's full."

"My middle name is Moon." Suddenly, it felt so easy to talk to Abigail, as if the breeze from the chickadee's wings had magical powers that had dissolved the prickly pit inside my throat.

"It's getting dark. How about we fill these?" She shuffled toward the seed can, then came back and stood beneath the feeders, handing me the scoop.

I added seeds, filling each container. Bob ran back and forth between us as if he was helping. When we finished, Abigail secured the lid and started toward her crooked shed.

"Do you want me to come back tomorrow?" I asked.

She raised a small hand. A yes, I hoped. Then she slipped inside. I heard the latch click. Bob barked.

"I guess we're done here," I said to Bob. But as we made our way toward Specter Hill Road, I felt the tips of my fingers where the chickadee had landed. And I smiled.

———•———

Mom's Fiesta still wasn't in the driveway when I got back. Inside, I fed Bob and got him fresh water. I was so sick of the cold, I couldn't stand it. I opened the door to the woodstove. Cecy had shown me how to light it. I needed to try.

I crumpled some old newspaper and placed small pieces of wood around it. I lit the paper, then watched the flame move to the kindling. Bob pushed in next to me, panting. When the fire took life, he barked.

"That's how it's done, Bob," I said. When the kindling was burning well, I added a few logs and shut the stove's iron door. Even though it would take a while to heat the house, I was already feeling warmer.

The front door to the house swung open.

"Wow, Ruby!" Mom stepped inside, carrying a foil tray. "You built a fire and I got dinner! I'd say this is a reason to celebrate!"

She placed the foil container on the table and grabbed paper plates. "I was hoping you'd visit me at the store."

"I didn't know where it was," I lied.

"You go by it every day on your way to school."

"Why are you all dressed up? Do you have makeup on?"

She grinned. "First day," she said, and shrugged. "I wanted to make a good impression."

As happy as she was, I was suspicious. This was how it started. Tomorrow, the classified ads would be spread across the table again. I lifted the foil. "What is this?"

"*Dawood basha*. Syrian meatballs. Mr. Saleem made them. He is amazing!"

Mom thought everyone was amazing until they fired her or had her arrested. I wrinkled my nose.

"Can you at least try it? I didn't have time to cook." Since we had begun our search for a forever home, Mom never had time to cook.

She scooped out the meatballs and some rice. It stained my plate red. "What's the green stuff?"

"Parsley. I think there's mint, too."

I nibbled a bite, then gulped down a bunch of water.

I made a face. "It's too spicy. It doesn't taste like meat-balls."

"It's lamb and it's what we have." Mom took a large bite and closed her eyes like it was the best thing she'd ever eaten. My stomach rumbled.

"How was school?"

"I need you to write a note."

"For what?"

"They're doing some Wax Museum. I need you to excuse me from it."

"Oh, I saw a flyer for that at Rucki's. Everyone in town goes."

"Everyone but us." I felt her eyes on me. "Anyway, we'll be gone by then."

"Gone where?"

Was she kidding? "Gone wherever. Our next forever home. We decided Fortin wasn't working, right?"

"Our next *forever home*," she said, emphasizing *forever home*, as if she didn't mean it.

"Yeah, our next forever home. Preferably warmer and with fewer arrests," I said in my best snarky voice.

Mom cringed.

"You have court next week. You said the case would

be over. We decided that when that was done we'd find a better place, right?"

Mom put down her fork and fixed her eyes on me. "Well, I'm glad you brought that up, Ruby Moon."

I flinched. I didn't want her calling me that. Not now. Not when I knew she was going to mess everything up again.

"I've been thinking. Maybe our problem is we don't give places a chance."

"You got arrested less than a week after we got here. And . . . don't you remember? You're the one who said *we haven't even unpacked yet.*"

She clasped her hands. "You should meet Mr. Saleem. He knows what it's like to have to work hard to improve his situation. He came here not knowing the language or anyone, and you should see what he's—"

"You always do this, Mom." I threw down my napkin. "When you want to leave it's all, *Go pack, Ruby, we're done with this place.* But now, you meet this one guy for one day and it's like he's more important than me. Nothing I want ever matters!" I jumped up from the table so fast the chair flipped over. I didn't care. I went into my room and slammed the door.

Bob scratched, so I opened it enough for him to slip in. I flopped on the air mattress. Any good feelings I'd had from feeding the birds with Abigail earlier in the day escaped in an angry puff of smoke.

I wasn't going to stay home alone, in this icebox of a house, waiting for Mom to decide, out of the blue again, that she was ready to move on to some new place that she picked without even talking to me. I was tired of never having any say in where we went or what we did. And I sure wasn't going to get stuck having to be in a stupid Wax Museum because Mom wanted to give Fortin another chance.

"No more fake forever homes, Bob," I said. If Mom wouldn't go back to the only real home we'd ever known, I sure wasn't going to make things easy for her here.

I'd almost fallen asleep when Mom knocked. "Ruby?" She pushed the door open and sat on the edge of my mattress. My body rolled into the sunken place next to her. I watched her look out the window into the night. Her hair was pulled into a ponytail, but ringlets had fallen out, framing her face. "It's almost eight o'clock," she said.

"It's too cloudy." My eyes began to sting. *Do not cry, do not cry, do not cry.* I took a deep breath.

"I'm sorry, Ruby Moon," she said. "You're right. I won't make any more big decisions without you."

I kept staring out the window.

"When court's done, if you want to move again, we'll find a new forever home."

"In DC?"

"Oh, Ruby." She sighed.

I sat up. "I want to go to court with you."

"But you'll miss school."

"Next Friday's a half day. They have a winter sports program. The school takes everyone to Okemo to go skiing."

"You could try skiing, too."

I rolled my eyes.

Mom shook her head. "Fine . . . I guess. This one time." She put her arm around me. "Cecy won't like it."

I shrugged. "That's Cecy for you."

Mom laughed. "I'd pick you over Cecy any day."

CHAPTER

6

For the rest of that week and most of the next, I kept my head down, resolved to stay invisible until I could escape Fortin.

That Friday, Mom let me miss school, as promised. When Cecy found out Mom was bringing me to court, she refused to go. "If you think it's a good idea to expose Ruby to all of those criminals, I guess you aren't interested in my advice after all, Dahlia," she said with her best sour-milk face. Mom was upset, but I secretly jumped for joy.

We pulled into a parking lot outside a large brick building. Thick black letters above the entrance read

VERMONT SUPERIOR COURT. I headed toward the front entrance.

"We have to meet with my public defender first," Mom said. I followed her across the parking lot toward what looked like a very old concrete house. Its outsides were yellowed and dirty. We stepped around a large bucket of sand and a shovel, and then Mom opened the front door and it seemed like we were walking into someone's living room. The floors were all wood and there was a giant empty fireplace.

"Good morning," a lady said. She had a long gray ponytail and glasses. She sat at a desk in the middle of the room. "You're here for Annie, right?"

Mom gave a weak smile and nodded.

"Have a seat." She pointed toward a small room with a couch and chairs. It was already filled with people. "She'll be right with you."

I took a seat next to Mom. Near us, a man in dirty sweats sat slumped in a chair, half-asleep. An elderly couple huddled together, holding hands. A thin woman sat in the corner scratching herself and shivering. A mom held a wiggling toddler. Next to her was a girl with long black hair and a bright orange coat. I recognized her as Melanie, the girl who sat behind me in

Mr. Andrews's class. I couldn't believe someone from school was here. Before I could look away, Melanie smiled at me. I crossed my arms and pretended to read a poster titled KNOW YOUR RIGHTS!

I did not like the sour smell in that room. I did not like the sadness that hovered over the people there.

"Ms. Stacks," a man called.

Melanie's mother stood, handing her the toddler. "Play with her while I talk to my lawyer," she said.

There was a tub of toys in a corner. Melanie led her sister over to it and knelt next to her.

"Here, Jess, let's do this one." Melanie pulled out a wooden puzzle and handed her sister a piece. The toddler put it in her mouth. "No, Jess." Melanie gently showed her how to fit it into the puzzle.

"Dahlia?" A tall black woman stood in the doorway. Mom and I followed her up a set of stairs and into her office.

"Hello," the lady said to me. "I'm Attorney Ralls." She winked. "Call me Annie."

Annie was tall and thin, with hundreds of tiny braids spun so high on her head they added another five inches. One of the braids was bright red and I couldn't help but follow that crimson streak as it wove in and out. She wore a skinny black skirt and a silky blue blouse.

She closed the door and took a seat at her desk facing us. She opened a file. "So, turns out Frank Chatty and Mayor Eton will be in court to speak before you plead to the state's offer."

Mom swallowed. "What does that mean?"

"The state's attorney says they're not necessarily objecting to you getting a reduced charge." She closed the file. "But Chatty, anyway, is the *victim*." Annie wiggled two fingers, air-quoting the word *victim*. "So he gets to say his two cents in court. Frankly," she continued, "I think they're trying to intimidate you and any other employee at the restaurant who decides to speak up against Frank Chatty. They want all of this to end, and rumor has it, they heard you've been talking to some of the ladies and stirring things up." Annie smiled as if this was funny to her.

"Well, of course I've talked to some waitresses. I know at least two women who saw how hard he shoved me! And he's done it before. I don't understand why they want to work for him."

Mom's voice was louder than usual. I watched her reach for her moon necklace.

"The thing is," Annie said, "to get this deal, you have to plead guilty to disorderly conduct. The prosecutor is going to read out loud what Chatty claims happened—that you shoved him, not the other way around. If you get up there and say you didn't do it, the judge won't give you the reduced charge and community service."

Mom shook her head. "You want me to say I did something that I didn't do?" Her voice was high-pitched.

"No, of course not. I'm just telling you that if you want to take advantage of this deal that guarantees you won't go to jail, then the judge will want to hear that you are sorry and it won't happen again."

"How can I say I'm sorry for something I didn't do? How can I say it won't happen again if it never happened the first time?" Mom's cheeks were pink.

Annie fixed her gaze on Mom. "We don't have to do this, you know. You don't have to take this offer."

"But what other choice is there?" Mom said.

"We can go to trial."

"So either I say I'm sorry and get the special deal or I have to keep coming back to court and go to trial and hope the jury believes me?"

"Those are the options," Annie said.

I lifted my head. "But if she goes to trial and loses, won't she go to jail?"

Annie nodded. "It's a real possibility. There are no guarantees at trial."

"Mom," I said, my voice choking up.

Mom put her hand on my leg. "No, no, I want to get this behind me. Behind us," she said. "I'll take the deal. I'll say I'm sorry and I'll do the community service. I'll do whatever I have to do."

Annie pursed her lips and nodded. "Okay, I have a couple more clients to meet. Head over to the court. We'll be in Courtroom C on the third floor. Have a seat there and I'll be over shortly."

We left the public defender's office and walked back to the court and got in line. When we were at the front, a man yelled, "One at a time." He wore a navy suit and a badge that read COURT OFFICER.

Inside, the court officer said, "Step through, counselor," to a man in front of us who was wearing a long black coat. The man put his briefcase on a conveyor that brought it inside a machine like you see at the airport. Another court officer watched a screen on the other side. The attorney stepped through the metal detector.

"Next!" the court officer said to me.

I stepped through the metal detector without a hitch, but when Mom followed, it beeped.

"Do you have metal on you?" the officer asked her.

Mom took off her belt.

"Remove your earrings," he said.

Mom stepped through again. The machine beeped.

The man pointed at Mom's boots. "Those have metal in them?"

Mom unzipped her boots. The people behind us seemed to breathe louder. Some looked at their watches. Mom walked through in stocking feet, looking like a shrunken version of herself. The machine beeped again.

This time the officer took out a flat wand that looked like a paddle. He waved it around without touching her. When it neared her chest, it beeped again.

"It's my bra," Mom said. "There's a wire in my bra."

My face felt hot.

The officer waved her through. "Go ahead."

Mom collected her boots and belt and jewelry.

"Next!" he shouted.

We moved to the side. As Mom got dressed, she shook her head. "No more," she said. "I will not let them make me feel like this again." She lifted her chin. "Come on, Ruby."

Mom and I took the elevator to the third floor. Now, with her coat off, I realized how nice she looked. I hadn't seen her this dressed up since DC. But even with her boots and belt and jewelry back in place, she still didn't look like Mom. Her shoulders were bent forward. Her head, low. I knew how she felt. It was hard enough to figure out where to go and how to act. We hadn't even gotten into the courtroom yet and I already felt tired. But I didn't want Mom to know that, so instead I grabbed her hand and squeezed it.

"It'll be okay, Mom," I said. "When this is behind us, we can move on." I flashed a smile. "We'll finally find our real forever home." I was careful not to say it would be in Washington, DC.

•———————•

Inside the courtroom, I kept my arms tight at my sides. There were rows of shiny wooden benches, like pews in a church. We slid into one of them. At the front, there was a giant, solid wooden desk that sat higher than everything else. I knew the judge sat there.

To the left of the judge's desk, a lady rifled through a pile of files. In front of the desk, a lady with headphones typed into a computer.

There was a table on each side of the courtroom facing the judge. A man stood behind one of them. "That's the state's attorney," Mom said. "Annie says he's very fair."

People waited in line to talk to him. Some were dressed in suits, others appeared as if they'd slept in their clothes.

More people entered the courtroom. Melanie, her mom, and her little sister sat next to us. I wouldn't look at her. I was worried she'd try to talk to me. I was worried she'd want to know why my mom and I were there.

A few rows in front of us, two men sat huddled, whispering to each other. One wore a police uniform. I recognized him as Prattle, the policeman who arrested Mom. The other man wore a plaid flannel shirt and had what looked like a white cushion wrapped around his neck. I knew he must be Mr. Chatty, the owner of Frank's Diner. I watched Mom stare at his back, her mouth in a tight line.

"I got waffles for breakfast," Melanie's sister said with a sticky grin.

"Hush, Jess," her mom said.

A court officer stood at the end of our row. "If she talks during court, you're going to have to leave, ma'am."

"Come on, Jess, let's color outside." Melanie picked up her sister and left. A man in a black suit and shiny shoes strode into the courtroom with a court officer. They were laughing and carrying on. I waited for the grouchy officer to tell them they had to be quiet or else they'd be asked to leave, too, but he never did.

Suit-man walked right up to the front of the court, cutting the line. The state's attorney pointed toward Mr. Chatty and Officer Prattle.

Mom leaned over. "That's Mayor Eton," she said to me. "He's the one who says he was at Frank's Diner when it happened. He claims Chatty never touched me. I heard he has a daughter in your class. Dakota, maybe?"

Mayor Eton sat next to the men, joining their hushed conversation.

A nervous feeling began pulsing through my body like an electric current. From the looks on other people's faces, they felt it, too. The skinny woman scratched. The man wearing sweats hiccupped. Mom hugged herself.

Annie strode into the courtroom through a back door. She was wearing a black suit jacket over her silky blouse. I watched her greet the state's attorney and take a seat at the front. With her crown of braids, I thought she looked like royalty.

"The judge is about to come out!" an officer shouted. "Make sure your cell phones are turned off."

There was a loud rap on the door and a woman dressed in a long, black graduation-looking gown entered. "Open court," she said as she took her seat.

The court officer banged a gavel. The sound made me jump. "The Superior Court is now open and in session. The Honorable Kathryn Doherty presiding. Good morning, Your Honor."

When the judge finished telling everyone their rights, the state's attorney stood up. "Number thirteen on the regular docket, State versus Dahlia Hayes," he said.

I shifted my legs so Mom could get past me. She walked to the front of the courtroom and stood next to Annie at the table. I started to nod my bangs forward but I stopped myself. If I disappeared, who'd be there for Mom? *If Mom can be brave enough to get through this, then so can I*, I thought. I bit my lip and raised my chin.

"Attorney Ann Ralls representing Mrs. Hayes. Good morning, Your Honor," she said.

"Good morning, Attorney Ralls."

The state's attorney stood. "We are here for plea and sentencing," he said. "The victim is present and would like to be heard."

Mom's shoulders slumped as Frank Chatty and Mayor Eton got up and stood next to the state's attorney.

"Mr. Mayor, surprised to see you here this morning," the judge said to Eton.

He chuckled loudly, as if he and the judge had a private joke. "You never know, Judge."

She did not smile back.

Annie looked at the table and shook her head ever so slightly.

"Mr. Chatty, did you want to be heard?" the judge said.

"Yeah, Your Honor." He looked down. "I didn't want it to come to this, but this lady"—he pointed at Mom—"well, it didn't happen like what she said."

Annie stared hard at him and I thought I heard him gulp.

"Are you wearing that cervical collar due to injuries you claim this defendant caused?" the judge asked.

Mr. Chatty touched the cushion around his neck as if he had forgotten it was there. "Yes, ma'am," he said. "This was all her fault."

Mom squirmed. Annie put her hand on Mom's back and whispered something in her ear.

"If I could add something," the mayor said.

"Are you a victim in this case, Jim?" the judge asked.

"Well, no, not exactly, but I was there and as mayor—"

"Well, I'm sorry, then," the judge interrupted. "This is not a trial. If you're not a victim, then no, the court does not want to hear from you."

The mayor crossed his arms. "Well, I think—"

"Can I have the file?" the judge said to the clerk.

Mom raised her chin.

I smiled inside. I liked this judge.

She read the file. "So, Mr. Chatty, to be clear, do you object to Mrs. Hayes getting the reduced charge and probation?"

"Well, I just think, you know, someone like her who comes waltzing into town and thinks she's going to do things her way, well, she should know that here in Fortin, you know . . ." He paused. "Well, she shouldn't be flappin' her trap about the rest of us folks who've been working hard here and serving this community for most of their lives."

The judge raised her eyebrows. "Mr. State's Attorney, do you wish to be heard?" she said.

The prosecutor flipped through a file. "It appears the defendant, Mrs. Hayes, has never been in trouble before. For these reasons we'd like to offer a substitute charge of disorderly conduct and probation."

I breathed a sigh of relief.

The red blotches had spread to the back of Mom's neck. But she wasn't looking down anymore. She was looking straight at the judge, her jaw tight, as if she was working hard to keep it shut.

No, Mom, I thought. *Don't say anything!*

"Attorney Ralls?" the judge said.

Please, Mom, I silently willed. *Please don't talk.*

"Well, my client does not concede these allegations. Nevertheless, she does wish to take advantage of the State's offer—"

"What does that mean, Attorney Ralls? Your client denies the charges?"

Annie turned toward my mom, who looked like she was about to burst.

"Yes, Your Honor," Mom blurted. "I never laid a finger on him. Mr. Chatty is the one who shoved me. He shoved me hard. I had bruises . . . and people saw him." She pointed at the mayor and Mr. Chatty. "They're the ones who are lying."

Annie turned back to the judge. "Your Honor, I think we won't be accepting the State's offer after all."

NO! I wanted to scream. *NO, NO, NO!*

Mom threw her shoulders back.

The mayor and Mr. Chatty started whispering furiously with the state's attorney.

"I don't see the need for that, Your Honor," the state's attorney said. "We agreed to reduce the charge . . ." He turned toward Annie. "Have you made it clear what she is facing if she goes to trial, Counselor?"

"I'll make it clear," the judge said. "Ma'am, if you go to trial instead of taking this offer, and a jury finds you guilty, you will face up to one year in jail and a one thousand–dollar fine. Do you understand?"

A buzzing started in my ears, softly at first, then louder and louder, competing with the beating of my heart.

"I understand," Mom said, her head held high. "I didn't do anything wrong. I am willing to take that chance."

"This will be a short trial," the judge said. "I'm going to give you a month to prepare. We'll start jury selection next Friday, January 21. Trial begins Monday, February 14."

Everything seemed to move in slow motion. Mom turned and walked out of the courtroom. I got up and followed. I think the state's attorney called the next case. Outside, Mom put her hand on my shoulder, but I wouldn't look at her. I nodded my hair forward and disappeared.

————•————

On the ride home, the roar of the Fiesta's engine competed with the pounding in my head. It gave me an excuse to pretend I couldn't hear anything Mom said. "Can you believe that man having the nerve to wear that collar around his neck when he knows I did no such thing to him!" she said. "Well, I'll show him." I couldn't tell if she was talking to me or trying to convince herself. I crossed my arms.

"I need to stop by Rucki's to see if Mr. Saleem needs help this evening," she shouted as we neared Main Street.

I gazed out the window.

Mom yelled louder. "It'll only take a minute but I want to get as many hours in before I have to take off time for the trial."

I made my mouth a tight line. Trial. Another thing I never agreed to.

"Can you believe the judge set the trial for Valentine's Day?" she said. "I guess she's not much of a romantic, huh?"

I couldn't believe Mom was talking about going to trial as if it were a chore she needed to check off her to-do list. I wanted to scream, *YOU CAN END UP IN JAIL, MOM!*

She glanced sideways at me. "So you're not going to talk to me?"

I looked at my watch: it was noon. The kids would be at the ski mountain by now.

"Ruby, I had to do it . . . and not only for me. I did this for you, too."

That almost got me to talk. *YOU DID NOT DO THIS FOR ME!*

"What kind of mother would I be if I let you see me cower to those . . . well, they're liars. That's what *they* are."

You'd be a mom who actually acted like a mom! I wanted to say. Even when it seemed like she was there, she wasn't. Not really. Ever since DC, it had been like I was the mother—making dinner, cleaning up while she went to bed early. I was tired of doing all the work but getting no say in what we did or where we went.

Mom pulled into a parking space in front of Rucki's. "I want you to meet Mr. Saleem."

Even though she had turned the car off, my ears were still ringing. I didn't budge.

"You can't stay here. It's freezing." Mom's voice had an edge. "Let's go."

A large poster was pasted onto the front door of Rucki's:

SIXTH-GRADE WAX MUSEUM
MONDAY, FEBRUARY 14, AT 6:00 P.M.
FORTIN MIDDLE SCHOOL AUDITORIUM
PLEASE JOIN US FOR THIS ANNUAL TOWN TRADITION.

"Hmmm," Mom said. "Looks like Valentine's Day will be a big day for both of us."

Not for me, I thought.

A bell tinkled as we stepped inside. Rucki's smelled of baking bread and strong coffee. Opera music played. Bins lining one wall were filled with carrots, sweet potatoes, and onions. Wide, wooden floorboards had been polished to a shine. A long counter ran across the back. A few small tables with chairs were arranged in a corner next to a wall with shelves filled with containers of maple syrup, jams, and fudge.

"Mr. Saleem?" Mom called.

Suddenly, Ahmad popped up from behind the counter.

"Good afternoon. May I help you, please?" Ahmad pushed his glasses up with his fist. "Hello, Ruby. You are not skiing, either?"

Mom turned to me with a smile I did not like. "Do you two go to school together?"

A tall, bald man entered through a swinging door in the back. He limped as he made his way toward us.

"Mrs. Hayes, how did everything go for you today?" he said.

I ducked into the chip aisle.

"Well, it's a long story, Mr. Saleem. How about I fill you in later?" she said. "Sorry I am here so late. Is there anything I can do to help this afternoon?"

"This is perfect timing," Mr. Saleem said. "I have many deliveries. You are here with your car?"

"Yes, of course." Mom turned, looking for me. "Ruby? Ruby, come here."

I slunk out holding a bag of Doritos, my hair in full protection mode.

"Ruby, this is Mr. Saleem." Mom stepped toward Ahmad and held out her hand. "I don't think we've met. I'm Dahlia Hayes, Ruby's mother."

Ahmad stared at her extended hand.

Mr. Saleem said something sharp to Ahmad in another language. Mom lowered her hand. Her cheeks tinged pink.

"I must apologize for my nephew," Mr. Saleem said. "In our country it is not custom for a man to shake hands with a woman. Ahmad thinks he is older than he is."

Ahmad stared at his feet.

Mom took a step back. "Oh, I'm so sorry," she said. "I didn't mean to—"

"It is nothing to be sorry for," Mr. Saleem said, smiling at Ahmad. "I remind my nephew that we are not in Syria. We are in America now." When he said *America* it sounded like *Amreeka*. "I remind him that here it is very proper for a man to shake hands with a woman."

Even though Mr. Saleem had just reprimanded Ahmad, he had a kind of sparkle in his eyes that made me think he was really proud of him. Mr. Saleem clasped his hands together. "Please, may I get you something to eat?" he said.

I thought about the Syrian meatballs from the other night. I shook my head.

"How about a sandwich with cheese and a Game Changer?"

I didn't like the sound of either one.

"I insist. Ahmad, please set the table for your school friend. Ruby can have something to eat," Mr. Saleem said. "And then Ahmad will walk her home."

As Mr. Saleem turned and began limping into the back, Ahmad set out a plate and napkin.

I pulled Mom aside.

"Ruby! That was so rude," she said. There was no sparkle in her eyes.

"What?" I said, blinking back tears.

"You know," she whispered. "He offered you food and you shook your head."

"Don't leave me here!" I gripped her sleeve.

"You know we need this job, Ruby. Don't start. These people are kind and Ahmad goes to school with you. He seems like he'd be a nice friend."

I hate this place. I hate this place. I HATE THIS PLACE, I wanted to scream.

Mom pulled away from me and disappeared through the swinging door. A moment later, Ahmad stepped through the same door carrying a grilled cheese and a steaming mug. I heard the Fiesta roar.

"Please." Ahmad directed me to a stool at the counter. "Sandwich with cheese and Game Changer."

I sat. He slid onto the stool next to me.

I sniffed the Game Changer.

"It is my uncle's specialty."

It smelled like hot chocolate. I took a sip. It wasn't just hot chocolate. It was the thickest, creamiest hot chocolate creation ever invented in the history of the world. I took another sip. It was as though someone had melted the best chocolate bar ever made and mixed it with cinnamon and nutmeg and Christmas. Each sip warmed me from the inside out. I didn't want it to end.

"This is amazing." I closed my eyes and let the chocolaty goodness fill me.

Ahmad smiled. "It is the Syrian spices that make it so good. When I first came to America, I missed my family. I couldn't speak English. Every day, I came home from school homesick for Syria. Uncle made his Game Changer to help my sorrow."

I ate in silence.

"You were not in school today," Ahmad said.

I shook my head. "Did I miss anything?"

"We watched a movie in Science. In Language Arts we did more research for the Wax Museum."

Nothing, then, I thought.

Mr. Saleem came out from the back. "Ahmad, you will walk Ruby home."

I wiped my mouth and stood. "I'm fine."

Mr. Saleem smiled. "I insist," he said with sparkling eyes.

———•———————•———

Outside, Ahmad walked silently beside me. I sped up. I did not want or need a friend in Fortin. I found it easier to move on to the next forever home if I didn't have people making me promise to text or call them. And I definitely did not want a boyfriend, ever. Ugh. And what if Dakota saw us walking together? I would never hear the end of it.

But no matter how fast I walked, Ahmad kept up, wearing his usual grin, even though we weren't talking, even though it was freezing and he'd be walking over a mile round-trip.

"Why are you always smiling?" I asked.

Ahmad jammed his hands into his pockets and shrugged. "I am happy to be in America. I am happy to go to school and meet a new friend."

"I hate school," I said. I thought about my last report card in Orlando. Mom never saw it or how I was barely passing. Why work hard at something you know you'll never finish?

"In Syria, there has been a big war," Ahmad said. "Every day, we were under siege. I could only go to school from six a.m. until eight a.m. In America, I can go to school all day. I am happy for this."

"You had a two-hour school day in Syria? Lucky."

"Not lucky. School must end by eight a.m. because the bombs started then."

"Bombs? Like real bombs that explode?"

"Of course." Ahmad kicked a piece of ice. "There was much fear for my mother."

"Where is your mother?"

"She is in Jordan now. But when we were in Syria, she was worried for me every day. Amu—that is what I call Uncle Mohammed—he was already here in Fortin. He told my mother, *You must come to Amreeka. It will be better here.* But my mother would not leave her sister, so I came alone. Maybe, someday, she will come. *Inshallah.* My brother, too."

"*Inshallah*? What does that mean?"

"It means, *If God is willing.*"

"Where is your brother?"

"Omar has found work in Turkey."

"Do you ever talk to them?" I asked.

"I talk to my mother every day on WhatsApp, but it is not the same as seeing her in person, you know?"

I knew. "What about your father?"

"My father is gone," Ahmad said, and his smile evaporated for the first time.

I tried to ignore the sudden hurt in my heart.

Ahmad opened his mouth to say something but then closed it. "The bombs," he finally said. "The bombs found my father."

I blinked hard, wishing I had kept my own mouth shut.

Ahmad was silent.

"I'm sorry, Ahmad." Before I even realized what I was doing, I heard myself tell him, "My father is gone, too . . . and I had to leave my home. I know it's not the same." I swallowed hard.

"When we had to leave Syria, everything happened very fast. We could only take the things we were able to carry."

I thought about how every time Mom and I moved, it seemed like we were able to fit less and less into our garbage-bag suitcases. I had begun to feel like I was leaving a piece of myself behind with each stuffed animal that didn't make the trip to the next forever home.

"What couldn't you bring with you that you miss the most, Ahmad?" I asked.

"It is not the things I miss. It is the people. We had a beautiful life in Syria. All of my family lived nearby. Every day I rode my bike to see my cousin Ali." Ahmad sighed. "Now we are scattered like seeds. Ali is in Saudi Arabia. Others are in Greece . . . Lebanon, Romania." Ahmad's forehead wrinkled. "I think it will be impossible for us to be together again."

I didn't know what to say. "You must have hated it here at first."

"One day, I tried to run away from Amu."

"Where were you going?" I asked. But I already knew the answer. Sometimes I wanted to run away, too. Where didn't matter.

He shrugged. "I don't know," he said. "I only knew that I did not want to be here. I thought to myself, *It is too hard here. Maybe somewhere else it will be less hard.*"

"So did you? Run away?"

"Amu saw that I had packed my things."

"Was he mad?"

Ahmad shook his head. "He brought me outside and showed me this little bird. A tiny bird with a black crown and gray feathers."

"A chickadee?"

"Yes, this chickadee. It was eating out of a feeder Amu had made. He said to me, *You see this tiny bird? If he can survive this cold winter in Vermont, you can, too.*" Ahmad smiled. "So I stayed. I decided I would be brave like this tiny bird."

Snow began to fall gently on us. I was glad for the distraction. I stuck out my tongue to catch a flake.

Ahmad laughed and copied me. "*Talj, talj*," he said.

"What?"

"It is a famous song. *Talj, talj, am betshati eddini talj. Snow is falling on the world.*"

"*Snow is falling on the world,*" I repeated.

Ahmad smiled. "*Friendship, prosperity, and love are falling like snow.* That is how this song goes."

"It's a good song," I said. We were at the bottom of my driveway. "This is it," I told him.

Ahmad bowed deeply. "Goodbye, my new friend Ruby," he said, grinning.

"Thank you for walking me home, Ahmad."

And even though that day had been about the worst since we got to Fortin, as I watched Ahmad catching snowflakes on his tongue on his way back to Rucki's, I couldn't help but hum his song to myself. *Talj, talj.* As he disappeared on the other side of the hill, I realized I was grinning, too.

CHAPTER

7

The next morning I turned over on my air mattress and squinted at the alarm clock. It was almost noon. I bolted upright in bed, feeling my heart beat faster.

Bob pushed open my door, his leash in his mouth. I breathed a sigh of relief. "It's Saturday," I said to Bob.

I tugged on my sweatshirt and stepped into the kitchen. "Mom!" I called, but only the rattling windows answered. The woodstove sat frozen and silent. There was a note on the table.

Ruby,

I had to go in to work at Rucki's. I didn't want to wake you. Cecy made Blueberry Buckle. I'll be home as soon as I can. Sorry the house is so cold. Cecy is stopping by with firewood later.

> *I love you, Mom*

Bob leaped up trying to grab the note with his teeth. I snatched it away.

I sliced a piece of the cake. It was the perfect combination of sweet and sour. I had a second piece and fed one to Bob. He kept licking the floor even after it was gone.

I thought about the long cold afternoon in front of us.

"How do you feel about feeding the birds?" I asked Bob.

His tail whacked everything in sight.

━━━●━━━━━●━━━

Cecy had found more warm clothes for me at Family Thrift. I dressed in snow pants, a scarf, hat, my boots and gloves. Outside, Bob hopped around me with his puppy grin as if to say, *Aren't we having fun? Isn't snow the best?* I felt bad, thinking how much he would miss these walks when we moved. Bob was the only one who seemed to like Fortin.

"You are a Froot Loop, Bob," I said.

We hiked down Specter Hill Road as a cold breeze gusted. A dusting of snow swirled in a mini-tornado. As I sped up to match Bob's quick pace, a feeling of warmth grew inside me. I raised my chin against the frozen air, feeling as if I'd won something.

At the bottom of the hill, I peered under the pine tree. No bunny, but the food I'd left was gone. I dug in my pocket and scooped out more lettuce.

Bob tugged on the leash, pulling me down Abigail's driveway. I still hadn't told Mom I'd been back here. But Mom was too busy with court and her new job to pay attention to what I was doing. When she was done with all that, maybe I'd introduce her to Abigail.

As we neared the campfire, I let go of the leash. Bob galloped toward Abigail, who was sitting on the bench with her head back. When she heard us, she sat up and smiled. It was the first time I'd seen her without all of her scarves. With her face fully exposed, she reminded me of a peeled apple that had been left in the sun, brown and spotted and wrinkly.

Nearby, a deer rooted in the snow. When the doe spotted Bob, it thundered away. Bob dashed after it, leaping like a wild gazelle.

"Bob!" Abigail commanded. He slid in his tracks, turned, then trotted next to her, panting and smiling as if to say, *I just wanted to play!*

"Good boy," Abigail said. Then she turned toward me. "I was about to head out on a hike." She lifted her feet to reveal two wooden ovals, like flattened baskets, one strapped to each boot. "Care to join me?"

"What are those wooden things on your feet?"

"Snowshoes. It's the only way to hike in the deeper snow." She held up another pair. "Would you like to try them?"

I nodded. Abigail put the snowshoes on the ground. I stepped into them.

"How did you get that deer to come so close?" I asked.

"One of my pets. She stops by for a good scratch and some corn."

As I watched Abigail buckle the straps around my boots, I noticed a name written across the snowshoes: LILLIAN JACOBS. I couldn't help but hear Dakota's voice in my head: *People knew she murdered them. But the cops could never pin it on her.*

Abigail handed me a pair of ski poles. "Try them."

I took a few steps, using the poles for balance. The snowshoes felt heavy and clumsy.

"Don't pick up your foot. Let the back one drag in the snow. You got it," she said.

Pretty cool. The snowshoes kept me from sinking.

"Let's go. I want to show you something." Abigail headed into the woods. "Keep an eye on Bob. I haven't checked the pond for new traps lately. Stay in my tracks."

"But what about the birds?"

"I usually feed them at dawn and dusk. We can take care of them when we get back."

Abigail tramped down a path, making it easier for Bob and me. The trees dripped with marshmallow-cream snow and the sky turned a deeper blue. It was so clean and quiet. Like the snow had sucked up all the hard sounds and left only the soft ones—the breeze ruffling the pine branches, the soft *chick-a-dee-dee-dee* of the birds, the swish of my snow pants.

She pointed at a tree. "See the yellow paint? It's called a blaze and it marks this trail. When you're hiking in the forest, always make sure you can find the next blaze; it will keep you from getting lost."

Bob trotted behind Abigail. Every now and then he'd veer off her path to leap into deeper snow. He looked like a seal, diving into it. When he went too far, she'd whistle and he'd fall back in line between us.

I watched her thin frame march effortlessly through the deep snow. She might have been tiny, but she was strong. We hiked deep into the woods. The yellow trail wound in a wide circle. If it weren't for Abigail and the blazes, I'd definitely be lost. My legs were getting tired and I began to fall behind.

"You need to step it up," she said. "It's not much farther."

Eventually, we came to a small clearing. It peaked in the middle and there was some kind of structure at the top. We hiked up the hill toward it. A trickle of sweat formed on the back of my neck. I loosened my scarf and unzipped my coat.

"Almost there," she said. "Stay in my footsteps."

As we approached the structure, I realized it was a bench made from tree branches.

"Who made that?" I asked.

But Abigail's eyes were fixed on the moon rising over the horizon.

I looked at my watch. It was almost four o'clock.

"It's a full moon," she said. "A perfect day for the Moon Bench." She brushed away snow and fell back into it. "Oh, that feels good."

It was like we were on top of the world. I slowly turned, taking in the scene around us. "What are those?" I asked, pointing at the horizon.

"The Green Mountains, of course. There's Killington Peak and Pico," she said. "That snowcap in the distance is Mount Mansfield. It's the tallest in Vermont."

The mountains rose and fell, dusty blue against the gray sky. The full moon hovered above them.

The sky was turning orange and pink and purple like it seemed to do in Vermont before the dark came. I fell onto the seat next to her.

The front legs of the Moon Bench were longer than its back legs, which forced me to lean back. I gazed at the rising full moon. It was so big and bright and close I felt as if I could almost touch it. It made me think of Michael Collins, racing toward it like a moth toward light.

If I were Michael Collins, orbiting the moon alone,

all I'd want to do would be to get back home. It made me think that being in Fortin wasn't much different from being on the moon. Everything I knew was so far away. Everything I was surrounded by was strange and different.

"Did you know that at the next full moon, there is going to be a Ruby Moon?" Abigail said. "That's what some people call a total lunar eclipse, because the moon can appear red." Her wild silver hair blew out in every direction, but her dark eyes were now as blue and peaceful as the mountains on the horizon. She seemed so much different from the shapeless creature I'd met two weeks ago.

"A Ruby Moon? Is that really real?" I asked.

"Of course it is."

"My dad used to tell a story about the night I was born. He said there was a full, bright red moon that night. He said it looked like a ruby in the sky, so my parents named me Ruby Moon." I closed my eyes and could almost hear Dad's voice. The Ruby Moon story had become my bedtime lullaby, but each time Dad told it, the moon got bigger and brighter. Each time he told it, I felt as if the moon had shone red just for me.

"Ruby Moons are very real. But rare," Abigail said. "They only happen during a total lunar eclipse."

"How does it happen?"

"If you look at the moon during a total eclipse, you'll see the Earth's shadow creep across its face. The shadow makes that part of the moon appear dark, like a cookie with a bite taken out. But the shadow keeps growing. Then"—Abigail paused, raising her arms to sweep the sky—"when the shadow has totally blacked out the moon, it changes. Instead of black, it appears red." Her gaze was fixed on the moon as if it was happening right before her.

"But what makes the moon look red?"

"Good question," Abigail said. "Even though the Earth is blocking the sun, indirect sunlight is refracted—bent—as it passes through Earth's atmosphere. When this happens, shorter-wavelength blue colors get filtered out, leaving the reds and oranges to light up the moon."

"It would be so cool to watch the Ruby Moon from here next month." I took a deep breath. "But we'll probably be gone by then. Mom and I are moving to our next forever home soon."

"Where's that?"

"Washington, DC," I said.

"Oh. That will be wonderful for you," she said, but right then her forehead became all wrinkly and her eyes went back to being as dark as a lunar eclipse.

I reached out and placed my gloved hands on top of hers. "But if Mom and I haven't left Fortin yet, maybe we could watch the Ruby Moon together." When she didn't say anything, I asked, "Who named this the Moon Bench?"

Abigail's eyes brimmed with tears. "My daughter," she said. "I used to travel to Boston for work. I'd be away all week and come home on weekends. But as soon as I'd get home, no matter what the weather, my daughter and I would come here to look for the moon. Even in the middle of winter."

As tears began to stream down her face, I tried to think of something, anything, to say to make her stop crying. I wanted to tell her about my dad. I wanted to scream, *I lost someone, too!* But my tight, scratchy throat wouldn't let me.

Abigail pulled out a rag and mopped her face. "We have to go before it gets too dark." With that she hopped up from the bench and started shuffling down the hill.

I stared at the empty space where Abigail had been

sitting and I saw words and a date carved into the wood. MOON BENCH, it said. LILLIAN ROSE, JANUARY 2, 1964.

When I realized Abigail wasn't waiting for me, I jumped up and followed. The woods were darker and colder now and I had to push myself to keep up. Bob was tired, too. He fell in line between us.

When we got back to camp, Abigail shuffled straight to her shed. The wind was gusting harder, knocking the birdseed containers together. "What about the birds?" I called after her.

Abigail removed her snowshoes. She made a swiping movement with her hand as if to say, *Forget it*. Then she disappeared inside and I heard the latch being hooked.

As birds gathered in the bushes, I removed my snowshoes and leaned them against the house with the ski poles. I stared at its boarded windows.

Stay out. Stay out. Stay out, it seemed to warn.

There was a crack in the plywood covering the closest window. I glanced over my shoulder, then stepped onto the large stone in front of the door. I leaned far enough so that I could squint through the crack. But all I saw was darkness.

Bob was licking his feet where the snow had caked. More birds gathered in the bushes. I returned to the seed can, filled the scoop, and made my way to the Chock full o'Nuts container. After emptying the scoop, I returned for more, but when I dug the scoop in, there was a *clink* sound. I buried my hand in the seeds and pulled out a metal ring with three keys. My eyes darted between the keys in my hand and the keyhole in the door.

Bob was by my side now. I pushed the keys back in with the seeds and filled the rest of the containers. When I was done, I secured the lid. I pulled Bob's leash from my pocket and attached it to his collar. "Come, Bob," I said.

Together, we ran from Abigail's camp, the full moon following us the whole way.

•————————•

When I got to the house, Cecy's truck was in the driveway. Smoke billowed from the chimney.

"Boots off," Cecy said as I shut the door behind me.

"Where's Mom?" I moved in front of the woodstove, standing as near as I could without touching it. Its heat wrapped around me like a blanket. The smell of roasting meat filled the house. My stomach rumbled.

"Mr. Saleem needed her to stay late and help with inventory," Cecy said as she opened the oven door and took out a roast. It was surrounded by baked potatoes. The pan crackled as she set it on the stove. I was dying to cut off a piece of meat and pop it in my mouth, but I knew Cecy would have a fit.

"Why does he need so much help, anyway?"

"It's hard for him to get around, you know, with his one leg and all, so it works out well. Your mom was lucky to get a job after her little show. She's not in a position to complain about working late."

I tried to brush off the prickly feeling Cecy's words gave me. I wasn't in the mood to get into it with her. I hung up my coat and stepped into the kitchen. I opened a bag of chips and shoved some in my mouth. "He looks like he has two legs to me," I said.

"I didn't cook this so you could spoil your appetite with junk." She snatched the chip bag from me. "One of his legs is a prosthetic. He was home in Syria with his family when bombs hit. Can you imagine?"

I swallowed hard, the chips sticking to my throat. I leaned into the sink and drank water from the tap.

Cecy gave me a look as I wiped my mouth with the back of my sleeve.

"What?" I said.

"Set the table, please." She started to hand me three plates, then paused, making her sour-milk face at them. "These need to be washed. Has your mom used the kitchen yet?"

"Cecy, do you know the lady down the road?"

She motioned for me to move out of her way. "Mrs. Jacobs?"

"Why doesn't she live in her house?"

"Did you see her?"

"She asked me to help her feed the birds."

"Dry this." Cecy handed me a plate. We hadn't used these dishes since DC. My stomach felt funny as I grabbed a towel and began wiping.

"Why does she live like that?" I paused to trace the plate's blue trim with my finger. I hadn't realized how much I missed the dishes.

Cecy shook her head. "I don't know, Ruby. I guess she's sad."

"Some kids say she killed her family in that house, and that's why she doesn't go inside."

"That is gossip fed by stupidity," Cecy said. "I love

this town, but there are some people here who don't have the sense God gave a goose." She held out another dripping dish. I took it from her.

"Abigail knows a lot about the moon," I said.

"Mrs. Jacobs? Yes, she should." Cecy stared into space as if she was trying to remember something. "She was some kind of computer scientist. One of the first, I think—a very long time ago—and did some work with astronauts or space or something." Cecy shook her head. "Lillian was always so proud of her."

"Who's Lillian?"

But Cecy seemed lost in thought, as if she had actually traveled back in time. "Mrs. Jacobs worked a lot. She commuted all the way to Boston. I didn't realize it at the time, but that was a hard thing back then, especially in a small town like Fortin."

"Why?"

Cecy gave a quick laugh. "It was a different time, Ruby. Some people believed women should stay home and raise kids, not jet off to work jobs they thought only men should do." Cecy soaped another dish. "Plus, the Jacobses were always private. Even before—" Cecy shook her head. "It kind of made her an oddity in town. People didn't get her."

"If she was doing something so cool, why didn't she tell everyone about it?"

Cecy shrugged. "I don't know."

I stared at Cecy. None of what she was saying squared up with the lady I'd met in the woods. "Are you sure we're talking about the same person?"

Cecy shook a wooden spoon at me. "Don't think you know someone because you met them once," she said. I felt a lecture coming on. "You know, women like Mrs. Jacobs paved the way for girls today, and it was no easy row to hoe. You, Miss Ruby, can enter any field you want—science, computers, engineering—because of women like Abigail Jacobs."

I grabbed three glasses from the cupboard. Cecy took them from me. "No wonder you drink from the faucet." She began washing those, too. "You know, my mother told me a story once." She stared into the sink. "Something about Mrs. Jacobs having a piece of an asteroid, or . . . no, it was a rock from the moon." Cecy nodded. "I think she said she had gone to visit and bring the Jacobses a pie and Mrs. Jacobs showed it to her. Imagine that."

Dad and I had seen a real moon rock at the Air and Space Museum once. I told him it looked like a stone from someone's driveway. *Oh no, Ruby*, he had said, gazing at it as if it were magic. *You can't talk about a piece of the moon like that! Imagine what it took to bring it here. If you held that rock in your hand, you'd be holding the moon itself.* He grinned. *Make a wish*, he told me. And right then I had wished I could do something to make my dad's eyes sparkle as much as that moon rock had.

"You know, it's funny." Cecy interrupted my thoughts. "I hadn't seen Mrs. Jacobs in ages and then, there she was, feeding the birds at the town green the other morning."

Cecy lifted the roast onto a platter and began making gravy in the pan.

"But what happened? What made her become . . . I don't know, it's weird how she lives."

Cecy shrugged. "After everything happened, she . . . well, she kind of disappeared."

"But what happened?"

Cecy opened her mouth as if to answer, but instead blinked her eyes a bunch of times. "It's good you're helping her, Ruby. That poor lady could use a friend."

Right then the door burst open and Mom struggled inside, hugging an old box television set.

In the commotion, Bob grabbed one of Cecy's boots and began jumping and dancing around Mom hoping she'd play tug-of-war with it.

"Down, Bob! You're going to make me drop this," Mom said.

"That's my good boot!" Cecy yelled. "Don't let that dog ruin my boot!"

Mom lowered the television. There was a newspaper on top. She tossed it onto the table and took off her coat. "Wow, it smells great in here."

"Where did you get that TV?" I asked. "It's so old."

"Mr. Saleem said we could use it. If I can get it to work, that is."

Cecy yanked her boot out of Bob's teeth. "That dog needs training," she said.

I cleared the newspaper from the table. The headline said: MAYOR PUSHES THROUGH FORTIN ANTI-HOMELESS ORDINANCE.

Cecy snatched the paper from my hand. "Eton has nothing better to do than drum up drama. Look at this new law." She read, *"Beginning February 1, it will be illegal to live in any structure that lacks running water and sanitation."*

"What does that mean?" I asked.

"Well, I don't have to tell you how I feel about him," Mom said as she washed her hands. "What homeless is he even talking about? If he wants to see homeless people, he should visit Washington, DC."

"I can think of only one person this affects. Your friend, Ruby," Cecy said.

"What friend?" Mom said.

I made myself busy draining the carrots.

Cecy squinted at the article. "I don't even think this is constitutional."

Mom smiled. "Ruby, do you have a friend you haven't told me about?" She put her hands on her hips.

"Ruby met your neighbor. Abigail Jacobs."

From the corner of my eye I saw Mom's smile disappear. I knew she wouldn't say anything in front of Cecy, but I could tell she was mad.

Cecy folded the newspaper. "Let's eat," she said.

"It's fine, Mom," I said. "Cecy knows her."

Mom gave me her *We'll talk about this later* look.

As we dug in, Mom said, "So far, this is the best part of my day. Thank you, guys." She smiled at me, and for the first time I noticed the wrinkles that used to go away when she got home from work were still there. She looked older and more tired than ever.

"Will you be working every Saturday evening?" Cecy asked.

Mom sighed. "If Mr. Saleem can use me. I'm trying to get extra shifts. Annie is going to start picking a jury on Friday," she said with a weak smile. "I'm going to have to take time off to be there."

"You're lucky Mr. Saleem is so flexible," Cecy said.

Mom nodded. "He knows what it's like to go through hard times," she said. "I'm grateful."

I took a bite of the roast and couldn't help but stare at my plate. It was all so familiar but so far away, too. I wondered if things would ever feel normal again.

●━━━━━●

After dinner, Mom cleaned up while Cecy and I brought firewood in from her truck. We stacked it by the woodstove. Every time we went outside I searched for the moon, but there were only clouds.

"What's so interesting in the sky tonight?" Cecy said to me.

"I was wondering if it was going to snow again," I lied.

Cecy looked up. "Don't think so," she said. "But you never know. You're in New England now, Ruby. Blink your eyes and the weather's changed."

I grabbed two more logs.

After Cecy left, I said, "I'm going to take Bob for a walk."

Mom was kneeling by the television set, a flashlight in one hand, a screwdriver in the other. "Did you go down to that lady's house when I told you not to?"

I hitched Bob's leash. "Cecy knows her."

"I don't care if she's Cecy's best friend. I told you not to go down there." Mom's voice was getting louder.

"What am I supposed to do?" I snapped. "Sit here alone and freeze to death? Plus, Bob needs to walk."

Mom stared at the blank TV screen. "You know I'd rather be here with you. We need this job."

"I've only been down there a few times."

"You went more than once?"

"Cecy says she's fine. She says the lady needs a friend."

"You don't know, Ruby. Some people seem perfectly nice at first . . ." Mom's voice trailed off.

"What happened to *Sometimes you have to have a little faith?*"

"Well, until I meet her, I don't want you down there."

"You're never home." I opened the door. "And she doesn't talk to strangers."

"I can see why you like her." Mom stood and handed me her flashlight. "Stay near the house."

I opened the front door, letting the blast of cold air chase Mom's angry words from my brain. Outside, I breathed in the night. The sky was as clear as if someone had swept those clouds away. The moon hung like a spotlight. I felt its pull, as strong as Bob tugging me onto Specter Hill Road.

When we reached the NO TRESPASSING sign, I stared down Abigail's dark driveway, wondering if she was sitting by her fire or tucked inside her shed. Bob sniffed the snow as I gazed at the full moon lighting the sky. "I'll see you on the moon tonight," I whispered. As we headed back to the house, I hoped Abigail was looking at it, too.

CHAPTER

8

"*Settle down, friends. I hope everyone enjoyed the* Martin Luther King Jr. holiday and teacher in-service day," Mr. Andrews said.

Bryce stood. "As Dr. Martin Luther King Jr.—for the Wax Museum, that is—everyone can thank me for the extra-long weekend." He bowed as kids clapped.

"Okay, Dr. King, save your speech for next month," Mr. Andrews said, his eyes crinkled in a smile. "We have much work before us." He held up a stack of index cards. "Today, you are transferring your speeches onto cards. This is all you will be able to refer to during the Wax Museum."

Mr. Andrews moved through the rows, distributing cards. "Most of your research should have been completed by now, but if you still have unanswered questions, you can grab a laptop from the cart." He paused by my desk. "Ruby? Do you need any?"

I shook my head.

"Your finished set is due next Monday, January 24. That is less than a week from today. These will be graded. Raise your hand if you need help."

I got in line to get a laptop. It was my only chance to use the Internet and I had plenty of questions, but they weren't about Michael Collins.

At my desk, I typed *Abigail Jacobs* in the search field. The article I had minimized last time came up.

FORTIN, VT. On March 4 at approximately 2049 hours, the Fortin County Sheriff's Office was dispatched to a report of a Chevy Impala that had struck a guardrail on Specter Hill Road. The operator, Abigail Jacobs, 37, showed signs of impairment. She was taken into custody and charged with driving under the influence of alcohol and negligent operation of a motor vehicle. She will be arraigned in Superior Court on Monday.

"Why are you always reading about the Bird Lady?" Ellen leaned over my desk. I closed the article and clicked on the NASA website.

Dakota popped up next to Ellen. Her large, round eyes blinked rapidly. "Didn't you know, Ellen?" she said with a smirk. "Ruby is the Bird Lady for the Wax Museum."

I kept my eyes focused on my screen.

Ellen shuddered. "Every time I see the Bird Lady at the town green, I get completely freaked out."

"Don't worry. Now that my father is mayor, he is cleaning up Fortin, just like he promised. He's getting rid of the Bird Lady. It's only a matter of time."

Trevor rolled his eyes. "How is your father *getting rid* of someone?" He and Bryce were sharing a laptop and I was pretty sure the only thing they were researching was a video game.

"Yeah, what is he, a mobster?" Bryce laughed. He nudged Trevor.

"It's not easy being responsible for a whole town, you know, Bryce. If you don't stay on top of things, then all the undesirables tell everyone how we're such easy targets here in Fortin and then their freeloading friends start showing up to make you feed them and stuff."

Ellen looked thoughtful. "I don't think anyone is feeding the Bird Lady. I saw her at Rucki's buying food."

Dakota shot Ellen a look.

Ellen's mouth formed an O.

Dakota narrowed her eyes. "I've seen the Bird Lady at Rucki's. I heard that guy gives her food for free. It won't be long before she's arrested for something. My dad says we need to remove undesirables, like the Bird Lady, from Fortin."

Ahmad seemed to wince at Dakota's mention of Rucki's. He opened his mouth to say something, but then shook his head and started typing.

"My mom says the Bird Lady used to be important," Bryce said. "She worked with astronauts or something. She even has a rock from the moon inside her boarded-up house."

I stared at Bryce to see if he was serious.

Dakota's eyes narrowed. "I heard that story. My mom says the Bird Lady made it up so everyone in town would think she's really smart." She sniffed. "She's a total nut job. People can't be allowed to live in a dirty shed with no running water and then walk all over town where everybody has to see them. It's too disturbing to watch."

Ellen nodded. "She's obviously a nut job."

"Well, my dad got a new law passed," Dakota said. "If she doesn't fix her house, she's going to get arrested. We don't need homeless people in Fortin." She flipped her hair. "It's only a matter of time."

"What's going on here? Is everyone done with their index cards?" Mr. Andrews moved next to Ahmad. Kids scurried back to their seats.

I clicked through photos on NASA's site, but thoughts of Abigail kept filling my head. I made a mental note to ask Ahmad if he'd met her at Rucki's.

It seemed like class would never end, but then Mr. Andrews finally stood at the front of the room pulling at his beard. "That's it for today," he said. "For homework, finish up with your research and be sure to check your school messenger accounts."

I never told Mr. Andrews we didn't have Internet. Or a computer, even. I closed the laptop and brought it to the cart. When I returned, Ahmad stood by my desk. "Ruby, would you like to eat lunch with me?"

I nodded. Even though I knew it would be hard to

make myself go inside that noisy cafeteria, sitting with Ahmad would be a whole lot better than eating my lunch in the girls' bathroom. It would also give me a chance to ask him if he knew Abigail. Maybe he knew something about this moon rock story.

●—————————●

At lunchtime, I stepped into the cafeteria. The smell of bleach and fried food made my stomach clench. I scanned the tables for Ahmad. But I only found Melanie sitting by herself. When she saw me, she stood and waved. I turned and walked out. If I sat with her, she'd probably ask about Mom.

Mr. Andrews came out of the cafeteria carrying a tray. "Are you looking for Ahmad?" He smiled at me with his crinkly eyes. "Did he forget to tell you that he eats lunch in my room?" He glanced at his watch. "You'll find him there."

I darted off. But when I got to Mr. Andrews's room it was empty. I had started to leave when the giant supply closet door opened and Ahmad stepped out. He wasn't wearing shoes. "Hello, Ruby," he said.

"What are you doing in Mr. Andrews's supply closet?" I asked.

"Praying," he said.

"In a closet?"

Ahmad opened the door for me to look inside. It was a large space. Any supplies had been removed. The floor was so clean it sparkled. A beautiful red carpet with gold tassels was spread in the center.

"Mr. Andrews cleaned it for me to use," Ahmad said. "It is my private prayer room. I read verses of the Qur'an five times a day. Here I do my noontime prayer."

"Why do you do that?"

Ahmad closed the door. "It is my religion. I am Muslim." He moved to the front table and put his shoes on.

I sat across from him.

"At first Amu told me, *Do not pray at school. You are not in Syria anymore. You are in Amreeka,*" Ahmad said. "But this is my religion. I will not forget I am Muslim." He looked me square in the eye. "Please do not speak about this to anyone," he said. "Especially Dakota and Ellen. They are not kind about things that they do not understand."

I felt my blood boil. "Did they do something?"

Ahmad removed hummus and pita bread from a paper bag. "One time, Amu called here to the school and the office sent his call to Mr. Andrews's room." Ahmad sighed. "I was not thinking and when I got on the phone, I spoke Arabic instead of English."

I peeled back the tinfoil from my pizza slice. "So?"

Ahmad swallowed. "Dakota reported to the principal that I must be planning terrorism because she did not like that I was speaking Arabic. So the principal called me to his office to ask me what I was talking about on the phone."

"Did you tell him?"

"Of course. I told him that Amu called to tell me he would be out when I got home from school. He called to make sure I had my key." Ahmad shrugged. "The principal was very nice. He apologized."

I shook my head. "Dakota is the one who should apologize."

Ahmad took a sip from his water bottle. "Why does Dakota keep saying you will be a bird lady for the Wax Museum?" he asked.

"I don't know. I live near this lady who likes to feed the birds. Her name is Abigail Jacobs, but the kids call her the Bird Lady. I guess Dakota and Ellen think I'm weird like her." I rolled my eyes. "Anyway, I'm not going to be anyone for the Wax Museum. I'm not doing it."

"You are Michael Collins," Ahmad said. "We are a team, yes?"

I shrugged.

"You must do the Wax Museum, Ruby."

I needed to change the subject. "So, have you ever met her? Abigail Jacobs?"

"Mrs. Abigail? Yes, she comes to Rucki's sometimes before the store is open, for coffee and supplies. Amu gives her seeds for her pets."

"Some people say she murdered her family," I said.

Ahmad shook his head. "No. Not Mrs. Abigail. She is a very kind lady. I think, when people are different, some people want to tell stories to explain this difference." Ahmad put his pita down. "Like the way Dakota did not like my Arabic. Instead of asking me what I had said, she made a judgment on her own. It makes no sense. The same happened to Amu when he first came here and people heard his accent. They didn't know him but they treated him like he did something wrong by coming to America." Ahmad shook his head. "So when I hear these stories about other people,

I think I will wait and meet them myself. There is always more to the story. Like with your mother, yes?"

Pizza stuck in my throat. I took a sip from my water bottle. I was not going to talk about my mother with Ahmad.

"Did you hear Bryce say that Abigail has a rock from the moon in her house? Do you think that's true?" I asked.

Ahmad shrugged. "Stories. Who knows what's true and what's not?"

I thought about what Dad had said that time we saw the moon rock at the museum. Would touching that rock be the same as touching the moon itself? The thought gave me a warm feeling. Right then I hoped that the moon rock story really was true.

⬤————⬤

When the last bell rang, I fell in among the piles of kids pushing their way outside. The steel-gray sky seemed to press back.

That's when I saw her.

At the edge of the parking lot, looking like a

shapeless creature in her patched coat and blizzard of scarves, was Abigail. Her hands fidgeted as she scanned the crowd. She looked like a kid who had lost her mother.

As kids bumped past me, I heard, "Hey, isn't that the Bird Lady?" "What is she doing here?" "Weird!"

I hunched my shoulders as I climbed onto the bus, but my eyes remained fixed on Abigail.

As the bus pulled away, Abigail's gaze suddenly locked on to mine. I stared back, wanting to hide but unable to pull away. I watched her mouth curl into a smile as her hand raised in a small wave.

"Stalker!" Dakota said. Ellen laughed.

I stared down at my own hands, wondering why they didn't wave back.

"Wait until I tell my dad she was at school," Dakota said.

•————————•

After the bus dropped me off, I ran to the house. I leashed Bob and headed down the road. Snow was lightly falling. When we got to the pine tree, the bunny was there. I watched her eat a carrot top as Abigail came hiking down Specter Hill Road. Snow coated her scarves like glitter.

"Why were you at my school?" I said when she got near.

She laughed a nervous laugh. "Lillian liked it when I walked her home." Her voice trailed off.

Lillian again.

She shook her head like she was trying to lose a thought, then slipped through the gate and started up her driveway. The smile I had seen at school was gone.

Bob and I followed. "Well, I'm here now," I said. "Do you want to snowshoe up to the Moon Bench?"

Abigail kept walking. Her body was hunched and small.

As we reached her camp, I made my way over to the seed can, but when I turned, Abigail had already ducked into her shed.

"Abigail?" I called. But the only sound was the latch hooking.

My insides fell. I stared hard at the door, wishing with all my might that it would swing open and Abigail would be there saying, *How about that snowshoe?* But the door stayed shut.

I filled the feeders. When I finished, I sifted through the can until I found the ring of keys. I turned them over in my hand and scanned the door, then I dropped them inside the seed can and replaced its lid.

"Come on, Bob," I said. As we moved past Abigail's shed, I paused. The wind whistled and I knew that quilt wasn't doing much to keep it out. A piece of faded fabric flapped in the icy breeze.

I wanted to tell Abigail I was sorry for not waving back. But at the same time, I wanted to kick the door and tell her to stop acting so weird. And I wanted to warn her.

Bob barked as if to say, *Come on! Let's do something fun!*

I tucked the loose fabric in place. Then I hiked up Abigail's driveway, feeling as frayed and useless as that shabby quilt.

CHAPTER

The next day, Mr. Andrews *stood behind his desk* rummaging through a bag. I saw him take out a baseball. When the second bell rang, he clasped his hands. "Good morning, good morning. Take your seats." He adjusted his glasses. "If you checked your school messenger accounts," he said, "you know that we are practicing Wax Museum performances today."

Kids groaned as Mr. Andrews moved the table to make space at the front of the room. I was too stunned. Of course I hadn't checked my school messenger account. We had no computer. We barely had a TV.

I stared at my desk. No way was I talking.

"Who wants to go first?"

I heard the rustle of arms being raised. Hopefully there'd be enough volunteers to get through the class.

"Dakota?"

Figures.

I peeked through my bangs. Dakota had placed a sparkling tiara on her head.

At the front of the room, she said, "I'm wearing this today, but I have a special gown for the Wax Museum."

Mr. Andrews crossed his arms. "I'm sure it will be terrific."

Dakota struck a pose with her hands on her hips. Her giant round eyes popped open. When nothing happened, she dropped her arms and turned toward Mr. Andrews. "Since we don't have a spotlight here, can you say go?"

Mr. Andrews gave a little sigh. "Go, Dakota."

Dakota sprang to life, making a swinging gesture with her arm. "My name is Lady Diana. I was born on July 1, 1961. When I was twenty years old, I married Charles, Prince of Wales, who is in line to be King of England." She made a sweeping motion. "I had two sons, William and Harry. I died tragically in a car accident in Paris on August 31, 1997, when the paparazzi were chasing me. I am beloved by all of England." Dakota curtsied. A few kids clapped as she glided toward her seat, beaming.

Mr. Andrews stood. "That's a fine *start*, Dakota. But you know you are going to have to dig a lot deeper than that, right? Okay, constructive comments?"

Of course Ellen's hand was first. "You looked like a real princess up there!" she said.

"Okay," Mr. Andrews said. "Anyone with a suggestion of where Dakota can improve? Ahmad?"

"Dakota has told the part we already know about Princess Diana," Ahmad said. "Maybe she can also speak about how it felt being the princess."

Dakota rolled her eyes. "Duh, she loved being a princess, Ahmad."

"Maybe, but it would be good to know something about her being in the light all the time. No one likes to be in the light all the time," Ahmad said.

"That is an excellent point, Ahmad," Mr. Andrews said. "Princess Diana was a very private person, yet was under intense scrutiny as a member of the royal family. Perhaps you can delve into those feelings, Dakota. How did she feel being thrust into the spotlight?"

When Mr. Andrews looked away, Dakota stuck her tongue out at Ahmad.

"I want you to dig deep into your characters. Anyone can learn statistics or rote facts, but you need to bring them to life. What did Princess Diana care about? What was her greatest failure? What brought her joy?"

Mr. Andrews walked over to his desk and picked up the baseball I had seen earlier. "I want you to think of your character like a baseball." He held up the ball for all of us to see. "I've already cut the outside," he said. He peeled away the ball's leather skin, then held it up again to show white string wrapped tightly into the shape of a ball.

"I'll bet everyone's played with a baseball," he said. "But did you ever wonder what was on the inside?" Mr. Andrews peeled away the layer of white string as if he was peeling an orange, then held up what was left. It looked like a ball of gray yarn. He pulled a piece of the yarn, then continued pulling and pulling.

"You're killing it!" Trevor said, covering his eyes.

But Mr. Andrews kept unraveling the ball until the yarn lay in a large gray mound at his feet. "With each layer, there are new discoveries." He held up a small red ball. "This is called the pill." He threw the pill on the ground and it bounced back into his hand. Some kids laughed. "But we're not done yet." He grabbed a pair of scissors and, using the sharp edge, peeled open the pill. He held up a tiny cork ball. "Did any of you expect to find this inside a baseball?" Most kids shook their heads.

"This is what I want you to look for in your characters," he said. "I want you to keep peeling away their layers until you find their cork-ball center." He set the tiny cork ball on the front table.

"Okay, who's next?" he asked.

I wondered what someone would find if they peeled away my layers. I didn't like that idea. Mom would be easy. She always said what she felt. Then I thought about Abigail and how her scarves were like her layers of yarn. Most people didn't even know what she looked like under there. They sure didn't know who she was.

"Ruby?" Mr. Andrews said.

I jumped. Everyone was staring at me.

"Ruby? Come on up."

What?

"You're next. Let's hear about Michael Collins."

What? I tried to swallow but the prickly pit in my throat had grown three sizes bigger.

Someone dropped a pencil. Kids whispered. I heard Dakota muffle her snort-laugh. Suddenly, Mr. Andrews was leaning over me. "Ruby, what's the matter? Come on, it's just practice."

The whispering got louder. I wished there was a trapdoor beneath me.

Ahmad turned around in his chair. "Please, may I go, Mr. Andrews?" he said.

Mr. Andrews looked at Ahmad, then shrugged. "Fine. Go ahead, Ahmad."

At the front of the room, Ahmad put his hand up to his forehead as if he was searching for something. Kids laughed.

Mr. Andrews sighed loudly. "Go, Ahmad," he said.

"I am the American hero Neil Armstrong. I am a very famous astronaut and the first man to walk on the moon. My friend is there, Mr. Michael Collins." Ahmad pointed at me.

I sank deeper, if that was possible.

"He was a good sport and let me and Buzz Aldrin take the lunar module, the *Eagle*, to the moon while he went to the far side that we can never see from Earth. After we came home, NASA made me a big celebrity. But I did not like being in parades. I escaped to my farm in Ohio. Some people say it's because I saw an alien, but really it was because I liked being an astronaut, not a celebrity."

Ahmad took a deep bow. Kids clapped.

"Okay. Who thinks Ahmad got to the cork center of Neil Armstrong? Bryce?"

"I think he did. He talked about his feelings and how people thought one thing about Neil Armstrong, but really it was something else. I felt like he was a real person up there."

"I liked that, too." Mr. Andrews stared at the ceiling and pulled at his beard. "It's also interesting how when people don't act the way we expect them to, we make up stories to explain their actions, and those stories are rarely true." He returned his gaze to the class. "Another comment? Dakota?"

"I didn't feel like we got to know anything about Neil Armstrong. That was stuff about why he didn't like to be in parades. What's that got to do with him being the first man on the moon?"

"Valid point, Dakota. More hard facts about the Apollo 11 mission would strengthen your presentation, Ahmad." Mr. Andrews crossed his arms. "You also need to consider the source of your information. Just because someone prints an article or writes a book doesn't mean everything in it is true. Although there were rumors that Neil Armstrong had become reclusive, and some speculated about the reasons for this, others have pointed out that he simply preferred a quiet life on his farm." Mr. Andrews lifted a book from his desk and handed it to Ahmad. "I meant to give this to you earlier. Neil Armstrong authorized this biography. It should help you separate fact from fiction."

"Thank you," Ahmad said as he carried the book to his desk. As Ahmad took his seat, he tried to make eye contact with me. I looked down.

"Okay, Melanie, how about you?" Mr. Andrews said.

As Melanie moved past my desk, her orange coat brushed against me. I wouldn't look up. "My name is Sonia Sotomayor," she said. "I am the first Hispanic and third woman appointed to the United States Supreme Court." As Melanie continued, I couldn't help but listen. She seemed different standing there pretending to be an important judge. She seemed really happy.

After a bunch of other kids went, Mr. Andrews said, "That's all the time we have today. Thank you to our volunteers, and I think what we can glean from today is we need more research. If you have too much emotion, get more facts. If you have only facts, find out why your person did what they did. Always make sure your sources are reliable." He lifted the tiny cork-ball center of the baseball and showed it to the class again. "Don't forget, you are looking for this. It might be small, it might be buried deep, but it is the heart of your subject."

Right then Mr. Andrews tossed the cork ball. My eyes popped open and my hand flew up. I wasn't sure if I was more surprised that he threw it to me or that I actually caught it.

"We have a little over three weeks until the Wax Museum," Mr. Andrews said. "We'll hear more presentations tomorrow." He paused and I swear he stared straight at me. "If you didn't go today, you should be ready to present tomorrow."

I looked at my hands.

"Index cards are due Monday. I will be grading them."

The bell rang. I left the cork-ball center on my desk and started to gather my things.

"Ruby, I'd like you to stay after class." I sat down as everyone filed into the hall. I avoided their pity stares.

When the room was empty, Mr. Andrews sat backward in Ahmad's chair so that he faced me.

I kept my head down.

"I spoke with your mom yesterday," he said. "She told me about what's going on."

My cheeks burned.

"You know, if there's anything you want to talk about, I'm a good listener," he said.

I wouldn't look up.

"If you want to stay after school to work on your speech or practice giving it, that's fine with me. I won't even listen if you don't want me to. You can have the whole classroom to yourself."

I shook my head. He didn't understand. No one did.

"There is no judgment in this classroom. Everyone does their best and I insist that we all support and encourage each other."

Right! I wanted to scream. *Have you not seen Dakota and her dopey clone waiting for me to mess up?*

"I know you're shy, Ruby, but I am asking that you give it a shot. I think you have a lot to say and I would love to hear it."

I peeked through my bangs at Mr. Andrews. His eyes were not crinkly at the corners as usual. They were serious as stone. He lifted the cork-ball center and handed it to me. "I want you to keep this, Ruby. I'm hoping it will help you figure some things out."

I took the cork ball from him, not sure what to do with it. "Thank you," I whispered. What I really wanted to say was *Why?* I tucked it into a pocket of my backpack.

"You are free to leave," he said. "But I am going to keep calling on you, Ruby."

My eyes brimmed with tears. *Do not cry. Do not cry. Do not cry.* I swung my backpack onto my shoulder, feeling its weight pulling on me. I stumbled down the hall, my body hunched forward as if the bottom half of me couldn't walk fast enough to keep up with my top half. I slipped into the bathroom and lowered the toilet cover to sit on. As I locked my stall, the bathroom door opened. I lifted my feet so no one would know I was there.

"Greetings, I am Ahmad. I cannot speak the English language." It was Dakota and Ellen. Their laughter ricocheted like bullets off the bathroom walls.

"Oh, Dakota, you do a hilarious Ahmad," Ellen said. "Why is he even still here? I thought you said your father was getting him and his uncle deported."

"My dad says the federal government makes it impossible to get anything done right," Dakota said.

"And what about Ruby?" Ellen said. "You said she was moving away, but she's still here, too."

"You didn't hear?" Dakota said. "Her mother got arrested. My dad says he's going to make sure she goes to jail. Now that my dad is mayor, he's cleaning up Fortin just like he said he would."

I almost fell off my seat.

"What?" Ellen said. "My mom told me to be nice to Ruby because she has a lot of problems. I thought it was because she never talks."

"I'd be sad for her if she wasn't so pathetic. Can she wear something besides that space sweatshirt? She looks like she shops at the lost-and-found table."

The door slammed behind them, muffling their laughter.

I hugged my knees. I wasn't leaving that bathroom until everyone in the whole school was gone. I didn't care if it meant missing the rest of my classes and the bus. I'd rather walk home than have to see those two again.

Sitting alone on that hard toilet seat, I had plenty of time to make up my mind. Now that Dakota knew about Mom, it wouldn't be long before everyone found out. Of course, Mom was too busy *speaking up for herself* to know what I was going through. There was only one thing left to do. Quit school. I bet no one would even notice that Ruby Moon Hayes was missing. By the time they figured it out, the trial would be over and Mom and I'd be on to our next forever home. Hopefully in Washington, DC.

After the last bell rang, I peeked into the hall. There was only a janitor left, mopping the floor. I grabbed my coat from my locker and stuffed everything else into my backpack. When I went outside, the buses were gone. It was like the whole school gave a great big sigh.

As I started for the house, my full backpack weighed heavy on my shoulders. On Main Street, I was keeping my head down, hair in full protection mode, when *bam*, I walked right into my mom's lawyer.

"Whoa, Ruby." Annie chuckled. She had been on her cell phone. "Maybe texting and walking should be a crime, too?" She wore a soft tan coat over her suit and tall heels.

I shook my head. *It was my fault*, I wanted to say, but the words stuck in my throat.

"I was going into Rucki's to find your mom," she said. "Care to join me?"

I nodded.

A bell jingled as we stepped inside.

"Hello, Mohammed," Annie called. "Is Dahlia here?"

Mr. Saleem stood behind the long counter. "She is running deliveries," he said. "She will be back soon." He placed a cup of coffee and a plate of dates on the counter in front of Annie.

She slid onto a stool. "Oh, that is just what I needed."

"How about a sandwich to go with it?" Mr. Saleem asked. "And a Game Changer for you, Ruby?"

"Sounds like dinner." Annie sipped her coffee. "This

is heaven." She turned toward me. "How are *you* doing, Ruby?"

I wanted to tell her about the Wax Museum and what had happened at school today, but my tight, dry throat wouldn't let me.

Annie bent her head forward and massaged the back of her neck. "What a day I had."

I knew how she felt.

"You know, tomorrow we start jury selection," she said.

Mr. Saleem put the steaming Game Changer in front of me and I took a sip, hoping it would loosen my words. "Thank you," I whispered.

He bowed and smiled.

"It's going to be a tough one. But don't count us out. Annie's got some tricks up her sleeve," she said.

Right then, I thought Annie was about the bravest person I knew. She was going up against Mayor Eton, Frank Chatty, and Officer Prattle and she didn't seem nervous. I couldn't even read from index cards in front of my sixth-grade class without freezing like a deer caught in headlights.

I stared into my mug. "How do you do that?" I asked, grateful the Game Changer had freed my words.

"Do what, hon?" She smiled as though she was confused.

"Stand up in front of everyone and talk."

She bit into a date. "Well, you know, I wasn't always like this. I was shy as a field mouse when I was your age," she said.

I didn't believe that.

"But I've always liked to help people." She turned toward me. "People who really need help. And when I did that, I discovered I could be brave because it wasn't about me anymore." She nodded. "If I didn't speak up, no one would hear their side. No one would know their story." She took another sip of coffee. "That's why I became a public defender."

"I could never do that."

"You think you're different from me?" Annie asked.

I nodded. I knew I was. "I get this peach-pit feeling in my throat when I have to talk. It keeps my words from coming out."

"You're talking to me right now."

"You make it easy," I said. "But we have this Wax Museum where the whole town comes. I'm afraid that even if I go, when it's time to talk, my throat will get tight and nothing will come out. Everyone will think I'm even more of a weirdo than they do now."

Mr. Saleem pushed through the swinging door. He placed a grilled sandwich in front of Annie. Ahmad was behind him, carrying a small pizza. "For us to share," he said to me.

"It's hard speaking in front of people. That is true," Annie said. "But I have a trick. You two want to know about it?"

Ahmad and I nodded.

She took off her suit jacket. "See this?"

"Yes," Ahmad said.

"Well, it's magic."

Ahmad pushed up his glasses with his fist. I wanted to roll my eyes, but I knew that would be rude.

"You're laughing at me, I know you are, but it is." She nodded. "When I get ready for work in the morning and I put my suit jacket on, I become a different person."

I lowered my pizza slice. "How?"

"As soon as I put on this jacket, I tell myself that I have the power to be the voice for each client who doesn't have one, and that makes it true."

"Well, my mom has a voice," I said. "That's what got us into this mess."

Annie leaned in to me. "Your mama did a brave thing, Ruby. Don't you forget it. You cannot *ever* be afraid to speak up for yourself. But now she'll be in court and that, well, that's like a whole other language she doesn't know. So that's my job now."

"What do you have to do?" Ahmad asked.

"Our investigator interviews witnesses and gathers evidence. Then I put it all together in a way that tells your mama's story in the language the court requires."

"And your jacket helps you do that?"

She nodded. "That's *my* magic," she said.

"Can I borrow your jacket for the Wax Museum?" I asked.

She laughed. "Nope. You're going to have to find your own Ruby-magic."

After we had finished, Mom still wasn't back.

Annie looked at her watch. "I have to get going. Can you tell Dahlia I'll talk to her tomorrow, Mohammed?"

Mr. Saleem nodded.

"How about I give you a ride home, Ruby?" Annie offered.

We said goodbye to Ahmad and Mr. Saleem and I got into Annie's car. It was cleaner and quieter than any car I'd ever ridden in. Annie hummed with the violin music playing on the radio. I stared at the side of her face. Her shoulders back. Chin up. I wondered if I could ever be as brave as her.

The moon seemed to follow us. It looked like a wobbly, lopsided egg. *I'll see you on the moon tonight, Dad.*

Less than a month, I thought. *We'll have this trial behind us and we can finally go home.*

CHAPTER
10

The next morning, I woke to Mom banging on my door.
"Ruby! You are going to miss the bus!" My alarm clock read six thirty a.m.

My door swung open and bright light stung my eyes. I wished I was a turtle who could hide deep inside its shell. My covers would have to do. I scrunched down.

"Oh no you don't." Mom tugged at my blanket. "You need to get up. Now!"

I felt the darkness creep inside me. My body was too tired to deal with any of this. Too tired to get up and too tired to go back to that horrible school. I hadn't heard Mom come home last night. I never got to tell her about my day or how I knew she had told Mr. Andrews our business. I never got to tell her how Dakota knew she'd been arrested or how I'd decided to quit school permanently.

Mom stood over me, fully dressed and with her makeup done. I squinted against the light. "Where are you going?"

"Jury selection starts today." She put her hands on her hips. "I had enough to deal with yesterday, and I get another call from your principal! I know you skipped class. Ruby, I can't take it. I told you, we are giving Fortin a real shot. We are not quitting this time, and that means you need to go to school. All of it!"

Her words prickled against my skin. "I didn't decide any of that." I sat up. "You did. I'm not going back. You don't even know what—"

Suddenly, the covers flew off the bed. Mom stared at them in her hands as if she didn't know how they got there. "I—I'm sorry, Ruby. I didn't mean to . . ."

But I didn't want to hear any more excuses. "You said we were going to make decisions together. I don't remember deciding it was okay for you to go to trial so you could end up in jail. I never said I was giving Fortin ANY MORE TIME!"

Mom looked as though I'd slapped her.

"What if you lose, Mom?" I said. "The judge said you're facing up to a year in jail. You always think everything is going to work out the way you want, but it doesn't. It never does!"

Mom spun away from me, her eyes wide. Black mascara tears streaked her face. She moved toward the door and stood with her back to me.

I buried my head in my knees, hugging them. *Do not cry, do not cry, do not cry.*

"I know I've made mistakes. But I'm trying to do what's right." Mom sniffled. "I guess it's time for you to do what you think is right." She closed the door behind her.

I flopped back, letting my head hit the pillow hard. I heard Mom put on her coat and say, "Bob, where's my other boot?" And then, "Oh, never mind, I'm late. I'll just get snow in my shoes." The front door slammed hard. The window rattled.

I blew air out of my mouth. I had won. But as the eerie silence of the house began to creep inside me, the prickly feeling returned. I slid off the mattress and pulled on Dad's Air and Space Museum sweatshirt. Bob pushed open my door and shook Mom's boot at me.

"Drop it, Bob," I said. But he carried it to the front door and scratched.

I ignored him and headed into the kitchen. I opened the fridge. Mom had finally bought the kind of orange juice I liked, with mango in it, and there were eggs and my favorite cereal. I poured milk over Frosted Flakes and started eating. Bob kept nudging me with Mom's boot, but every time I tried to grab it, he scurried toward the door and scratched.

It felt weird not hurrying to school. I thought about the kids filing into Mr. Andrews's class. There would be more presentations. More comments. I imagined Ahmad, smiling as he scanned the halls for me. I imagined his smile disappearing when he realized I wasn't there.

It wasn't my problem. Ahmad needed to make friends with someone else. Even though he'd already been in Fortin for two years and he hadn't done a very good job so far.

"I'm so done with that place," I said to Bob. But my smile disappeared, too.

Bob dropped the boot, then put his paws on the table, craning his neck to reach the leash.

"Down, Bob!" I grabbed it. "Okay—okay, let's go." I

dressed in my snow pants and hat. Why not go for a big walk? I had all day. I wrapped a scarf around my face, slipped into my boots, and grabbed a pair of gloves. Before we left, I shoved two handfuls of lettuce in my pocket.

———•———

Fat snowflakes fell from the sky as Bob and I made our way down Specter Hill. The road was already covered in a blanket of white. Everything looked so clean. I pulled my scarf tight. Fortin never seemed to cancel school. I tried to shake off the nagging feeling that I should be there instead of here. Flakes gathered on my coat.

"Quitting school is the right decision," I said to Bob. Maybe a magic jacket worked for Annie but I had no magic.

At the bottom of the hill, the bunny sat in the middle of the road as if she was lost. I walked up to her, but she stared straight ahead.

"You're not invisible, little bunny. I can see you."

I stared past the NO TRESPASSING sign and felt a pang. I hadn't helped Abigail feed the birds yesterday. But the way she'd disappeared into her shed last time had made me feel like she didn't really want me around. I turned my attention back to the bunny. "You can't stay there," I said. Bob whined as I hooked his leash on a branch. I bent down to pick up the bunny, but she hopped under the pine tree. I followed and dumped out the lettuce. "Where's your family, little bunny?" I asked.

"She was probably someone's pet."

I jumped at Abigail's voice. "Where did you come from?" I asked.

"The town green."

"Do you feed the birds there every morning?"

"Well . . ." Abigail hugged herself and smiled. She shook her head. "I used to, a long time ago, with my daughter." She stared down her driveway as if there were someone standing there waiting for her. Then she turned back to me. "After you started helping me, I remembered how much I missed it." Abigail crouched down. The bunny hopped near her. "Most cottontails only come out at dawn and dusk," she said. "This one doesn't seem to have her instincts in order." She looked at me. "Do you want to pet her?"

"She won't let me get near."

"Try again," Abigail said. "She likes to be scratched behind the ears."

I removed my glove and cautiously knelt next to Abigail. The bunny didn't hop away. I ran my fingers through her fur. It felt like strands of fine, cold silk.

"Did you know cottontails can literally be scared to death? Scared so bad they die. Right on the spot," Abigail said.

I thought about school and the Wax Museum. "I know how they feel."

"Me too." Abigail showed her gap-toothed smile. And when she did that, the heavy feeling I'd been carrying since yesterday's Wax Museum practice vanished, as if Abigail had said, *Here, let me take that for you.* I felt lighter than I had in days.

"Scrappy," I said.

"What's that?"

"I'm going to name her Scrappy, because you have to be scrappy to live in these woods."

"That you do," Abigail said, and she laughed.

The snow was falling heavier now. Maybe there would be an early dismissal. I sure didn't want to be on the road when the bus came by.

I waited for Abigail to ask me why I hadn't come yesterday or why I wasn't in school. Instead she said, "You know, today is a perfect day for flying."

"What do you mean?"

"I can show you if you have time."

I nodded.

When we reached her camp, Abigail retrieved the snowshoes and handed them to me. "I know the perfect place," she said.

I strapped on the snowshoes and grabbed a pair of poles, wondering what we were really doing. Bob leaped in the air, trying to catch every single flake in his mouth. Every now and then he'd bark at the snow as if to say, *Slow down, I can't keep up!*

"Follow me!" Abigail said.

She set out in a direction opposite from last time. Bob and I followed. Snow fell around us, but the forest's pine-branch canopy acted like a shield. We hiked in silence. I breathed. The trees stood silent guard. I stared at their massive trunks and wondered how long they had lived there, growing and protecting.

A line of bark bulged up the side of one tree like a thick rope. "What's this?" I asked.

"Sugar maple."

I took off my glove and felt it—rough, but sturdy and strong. Nothing was going to knock it down.

"What caused this?" I asked, pointing to the rope-like bulge that ran up the entire tree.

"It was hit by lightning. That bulge shows the bolt's path from tip to root."

It was hard to imagine the power of a lightning bolt running the length of this tree. Yet here it stood, scarred but alive. I gave it a grateful pat.

We continued hiking until I was so warm I had to unzip my coat. My muscles burned and I was about to ask if we could take a rest when Abigail said, "This is it."

We exited the protection of the forest and hiked into a snow-filled field that seemed to stretch forever. There wasn't a branch, or rock, or anything breaking up its colorless blanket. In the middle, there was a hill with a gradual slope. Abigail snowshoed toward its peak. At the top, she lifted her face and arms to the sky, and it made me think of the sugar maple tree—scarred but still standing. When I caught up to her, she had this content look on her face that reminded me of how Dad looked on a day off, when it was just us in our pajamas settling in to do a puzzle.

"Ready?" she asked. Then she plopped down, butt first, lying in the heavy snow as if she was going to make a snow angel. "Come on, try it!"

I copied her, falling back, letting the fat, heavy snowflakes fall on my face. I giggled.

"Now put your hands up to the sides of your face. In front more. Try to keep your palms flat, making like a tunnel so you can only see up. That's it. Now stare into the sky."

I did as she said, concentrating on the cotton-ball snow falling directly at me like a meteor shower. Suddenly, my body felt as if it were slowly rising. Up, up, up. Levitating like in a magician's trick. Higher and higher. But I didn't have time to be scared because it felt right and wonderful. I was so light and free. Floating toward space. And I couldn't help but laugh when I heard Abigail sing:

Come, Josephine, in my flying machine
Going up, she goes, up she goes
Balance yourself like a bird on a beam
In the air she goes, there she goes
Up, up, a little bit higher
Oh my, the moon is on fire

Come, Josephine, in my flying machine
Going up, all on, goodbye

Then Abigail started laughing, too. We laughed and sang because we felt so good soaring and singing through that snowstorm, and maybe no one else would understand because most people try to get *out* of the snow, but Abigail and I did, and we had a secret now. We could fly.

Finally, Abigail sat up, laughing and breathing hard. Her scarves had slipped back, revealing her wrinkly apple skin. "Ohhh, that was wonderful. I haven't done that in ages," she said.

"That was so cool! How did you make it feel like we were really flying?" I asked, but I already knew the answer. Abigail was magic.

"Well, most people don't have the patience to try. But really, it's perspective. When you put your hands up to the sides of your face, you block out your peripheral vision. When you focus only on the falling snow, you feel like your body is rising."

"Kind of like the time when I was sitting in our Fiesta while Mom was in the grocery store and the car next to us started backing up. And I got scared because

I thought our car was rolling forward until I looked over and saw the other car was moving, not us."

"Your perspective can change everything," she said.

And I knew it was true. In the other schools I'd been to in the last two years, it had never bothered me to skip school. But missing today continued to nag at me.

"Penny for your thoughts?" Abigail said.

I don't know if it was because I felt safe out there in the middle of that snow-filled field. Maybe it was because my brain had started to freeze. But I told Abigail all about Mom and getting arrested and how scared I was that she was going to disappear on me, too.

"Ever since we left DC," I said, "Mom keeps saying everything is going to work out when it never does. It's like she doesn't see the bad stuff until it's real bad, and then she wants to pack and move." I scooped up a handful of snow and formed it into a ball. "And she gets to make all the decisions . . . where we go, when we leave, when we don't. Nothing I want matters."

"Have you told her how you feel?"

I didn't answer.

Abigail nodded. "Well, that would be a good place to start."

I turned toward Abigail and suddenly she seemed smaller to me, as if the worries I had unloaded were now weighing her down.

"I know it doesn't seem fair," she said. "But your mom is trying to do what she thinks is best."

"I guess. Sometimes I wish I could be more like her. She's not afraid to say anything to anyone. She never worries that people will think what she says is dumb." I tossed my snowball and watched it disappear into the heavy snow. "I could never be that way."

"There is a power to quiet, too." Abigail pulled off her scarf and rewrapped it. "The problem comes when you don't speak at all. Then you're letting someone else tell your story." She stared at her snow-covered boots. "No one knows that better than me."

Snowflakes collected on our clothes and hair and I wondered how long it would be before we were completely buried. I wondered whether anyone would even notice. Then I shook my head, sending the flakes flying. Mom would notice. Cecy would notice. Ahmad would notice.

"I'm supposed to be in school today," I said. "But there's this Wax Museum, and I'm . . . I can't do it."

"Ah, the famous Wax Museum." Abigail pulled a

paper bag from her sack. "Rye bread with butter?" she asked. I hadn't realized how hungry I was until she handed it to me. "Who are you going to be?"

"Michael Collins. One of the astronauts from Apollo 11."

"Oh, I know Mike."

"You've heard of him?"

"No. I know him."

"You know the astronaut Michael Collins? Like, you've met him?"

"I worked with Mike and Buzz and Neil."

I stared at her while she brushed bread crumbs off her pants. Even though Cecy had told me what she remembered about Abigail from when she was little, I was still having a hard time matching that Abigail Jacobs with the Abigail I knew.

She noticed me staring. "You don't believe me."

"I . . . Well . . . um, that's a big deal. You . . . What did you do?"

Abigail winced, as if it physically hurt her to remember. I worried I'd asked too many questions and she was going to disappear on me again. But after a moment she said, "Back in the sixties and seventies, I worked with some of the first computers."

"What did you do?" I asked again.

"I wrote code." Abigail stared blankly into the gray sky. "Computers were still relatively new and I was fascinated by them. Software engineering classes didn't even exist yet. I learned everything on my own, then applied to work as a computer programmer in Boston. It was a long drive from here, but we needed the money and the facility I applied to work at needed labor, so they were willing to hire women." She gave me a knowing look. "They weren't always so generous with us. Anyway, soon after I started, we got a contract with NASA." She smiled. "It was thrilling. We worked long hours, but it was my team that wrote the code that instructed the *Eagle* first to land on the moon, and then launched it to rendezvous with the *Columbia*."

I didn't know what to say. I had seen lots of photos of the scientists who worked on the Apollo 11 moon landing. They always showed groups of men with thick glasses and short-sleeved shirts and ties. There were no women. There was no Abigail Jacobs.

"Why doesn't anyone know about this?" I asked.

"Well, you know I'm not much of a talker." She shrugged. "But the real reason is that it was top secret. I had high-level security clearance. The United States was in a competitive space race with the Soviet Union then. To discuss anything outside of work would have been treason. Even my husband didn't know what I was working on."

I really wanted to believe Abigail. I had heard about women like Dorothy Vaughan, Mary Jackson, and Katherine Johnson, who helped put the first men in space. No one knew about them until the book *Hidden Figures*. But if people had finally learned about them, why didn't anyone know about Abigail? I had researched her name in every possible way, but nothing ever came up about a computer programmer named Abigail Jacobs.

Then I remembered one piece of evidence that could confirm her story.

"Do you have a moon rock in your house?" I asked.

"So they *are* still talking about me." She gave a weak smile. "None of that matters anymore. It's almost like it never happened."

We sat in silence eating our bread and butter. Then in a soft voice Abigail said, "You know, Ruby, if you'd like, you can practice your Wax Museum speech in front of me."

I shook my head. But I thought about how easy it

was to talk to Abigail. I thought maybe if she came to the Wax Museum, and sat in the front and I stared straight at her and pretended I was only talking to her . . . I took a deep breath. "If I did the Wax Museum, would you come?"

Abigail's eyes darkened and the sadness seemed to wrap around her like her layers of scarves. After a few moments she mumbled, "Oh—oh dear. With everyone in town? At the school? No. No, I can't . . ." She popped up. "We need to go," she said. She snowshoed toward the woods. Bob followed immediately, diving in and out of the snow like a seal.

I stood, giving the gray sky one last glance. My face felt hot and I bit my lip. Why did my words always ruin everything? I hurried to catch up, worried Abigail was on her way back to her shed so she could lock herself inside and disappear.

As we hiked in silence, the snow turned to light flurries. After another hour or so of silence, I finally looked around and realized we'd made our way to the hill with the Moon Bench.

"How about a rest before we head back?" Abigail said as she fell onto the bench.

It was late afternoon. The storm was over and the

setting sun stretched across the mountains in the distance. Even though we had hiked all day, I wasn't in any hurry to return to an empty house or face Mom.

I fell onto the bench next to Abigail.

I don't know if it was our hike or flying in the snowstorm, or if there was just something about the Moon Bench, but right then, I knew that I had to make a decision—either quit school or do the Wax Museum. And if I did the Wax Museum, the laughter and whispers would continue. If I did it, no matter how hard I worked, I'd probably still mess up.

Having to make this decision made me angry.

I was angry at Dad for leaving us. Angry at Mom for getting arrested. Angry at Mr. Andrews for making it so hard to get out of his stupid Wax Museum. Tears tried to escape, but I held my breath and squeezed my eyes tight.

But as mad as I was, a thought kept pushing its way into my head.

Maybe there was more than being silent and invisible. Maybe, down deep, I could be like Mom and Annie. Maybe I did have a voice.

Sitting high above the world, with the sun resting on top of the mountains, I began to feel like I really had traveled into space. The sky was turning pink and orange and purple and all those colors swirled around me and through me until they were part of me. I tried to look away, but I couldn't, and that made me even madder because I didn't want to be part of something so beautiful when I felt so ugly.

I leaned in to Abigail. She put her arm around me and combed my hair with her fingers. Then in a whisper she breathed my name: "Ruby Moon."

I lifted my chin to look into her watery eyes.

"If you speak at the Wax Museum, Ruby, I will come."

And I nodded because I knew how hard that would be for her, but I knew she would do it for me. And I thought, if Abigail could do that, then maybe I could, too. Maybe I could be brave enough to travel to the far side of the moon. Maybe I could be brave enough to speak in front of all those people.

The sun fell below the earth and the black grew and grew until the beautiful streaks of purple and orange and pink gave way to the dark. Without a word, Abigail stood and I followed her back to camp.

CHAPTER

11

I spent the weekend writing my Wax Museum index cards. Mom didn't mention our fight or the fact that I skipped school. But she seemed really happy when I asked her to drive me to Fortin's Babcock Library to check out every book on Michael Collins and Apollo 11. She was even happier Sunday night when I packed my backpack for school. She must have told Cecy about it, because she came over with homemade chicken soup and kept asking if it made me feel better, which it kind of did.

On Monday morning, I brought in the best set of index cards I could come up with. As I handed them in, Mr. Andrews gave me a smile and a quick nod. "Welcome back, Ruby," he said with his crinkly eyes. "We missed you on Friday."

When he'd collected cards from every student, he told us, "I will work diligently on these and hope to get them back to you by the end of next week for final revisions."

Kids groaned.

"Today we are going to work on costumes," he said. "Start by sketching your outfit. You'll need to brainstorm items that will bring your character to life. If you're Malala Yousafzai, what do your clothes look like? What did Neil Armstrong and Michael Collins bring to the moon? What does Sonia Sotomayor need for court? Princess Diana, how will you wear your hair?"

"Oh, I already know, Mr. Andrews." Dakota beamed.

Of course she does, I thought.

"We have three weeks until the Wax Museum. It will go faster than you think, so let's begin."

•————————•

Over the next week, Mom stayed busy. When she wasn't working or meeting with Annie or trying to convince the waitresses to stand up to Chatty, she was too tired to even ask what I was doing. She didn't know that I was spending every afternoon snowshoeing and feeding the birds with Abigail. As much as I loved spending time with Abigail, inside I was counting the days until the trial was over and we could move back to our real forever home in Washington, DC.

On the last day of January, I headed to Abigail's after school as usual, but when Bob and I reached the NO TRESPASSING sign, I froze. A police cruiser sat parked at the bottom of her driveway, motor running. Exhaust poured from its tailpipe.

I sped toward Abigail's camp, skidding in the fresh snow, Bob at my heels. When we reached the campfire, I was immediately relieved to see that Abigail wasn't hurt. But something was wrong. She stood in front of her boarded-up house, wrapped in her scarves, arms crossed. Even with only a sliver of her face exposed, I could see anger flashing from her eyes at the officer, who I recognized as Prattle. Bob barked.

Prattle spun toward me. "Hold that dog!" He clutched a piece of paper and a hammer. I gripped Bob's leash. Prattle spoke to Abigail. "It's a new law," he said, pointing the hammer at the boarded-up house. "I need to go inside to see if it's livable. I need to make sure you have running water and working electricity."

Abigail fidgeted with her scarves.

"Okay, I guess we'll have to do this the hard way." Prattle took an awkward step onto the wide stone. His feet sank into the snow. He nailed the paper to the front door. In bold letters it read: NOTICE OF CONDEMNATION. With each blow of the hammer, the house shook.

"You have two weeks to either let us inspect this house to make sure it's livable or you need to vacate the premises," he said. "If you don't, you'll be subject to fine and arrest."

I wanted to tell him to stop. I wanted to tell him that she was perfectly fine the way things were. Instead, I tugged on Bob's leash and ducked behind Abigail.

"Who are you?" Prattle squinted at me.

I stared at my boots, letting my hair fall forward.

"Ruby helps me feed the birds," Abigail said.

Prattle shook his head. "Well, maybe you can talk some sense into her," he said to me. Then he turned and headed up the driveway toward his cruiser.

Abigail's head dropped and I was sure she was about to disappear on me. Instead she said, "How about a snowshoe?"

●————————●

As we headed into the forest I glanced over my shoulder, half-expecting Officer Prattle to return.

"Aren't you worried?" I asked.

"Worried about what?"

"Worried about what just happened. They're going to arrest you if you don't fix your house and move out of your shed."

Abigail shook her head. "They can't," she whispered.

Even though it was freezing, my face felt hot.

"Abigail, why won't you live in your house?"

Abigail kept hiking.

"Where is your family?"

I thought about all the things Abigail and I had talked about: the moon, which seeds the chickadees liked best, how much she loved waking up to deer sleeping outside her shed. But, as if we had some unspoken rule, I had never asked her about her house, or about Dakota's story, or about the name staring up at me from my snowshoes: LILLIAN JACOBS.

Abigail hiked harder and faster. I tried to keep up.

"There must be someone else who knows about the work you did on Apollo 11? How come I can't find anything on the Internet or in any books? How come no one else knows about a computer scientist named Abigail Jacobs?"

Abigail wasn't hiking anymore. She was staring into the woods. "I was on my way home from Boston when it happened. I . . . I didn't know . . ."

"When what happened?"

"The nor'easter. They must have gone out to look for me," she whispered. "It was all my fault. They must have thought I had gotten stuck. It was snowing so hard. And the ice."

"Who? Who was looking for you?"

"And then there was nothing. For two months I waited for—for . . . something. Anything. People wanted answers. I had no answers."

"Who wanted answers, Abigail?" I hiked until I faced her, but her eyes were dark and unfocused.

"Abigail!" I yelled. "You need to move into your

house. That officer . . . he's going to return. People in town say bad things about you because they don't know you. They think you can't take care of yourself. They think you're dangerous."

Abigail pivoted from me and began snowshoeing toward camp. "I can't do it," she mumbled. "I can't."

"Abigail, do you really have a rock from the moon?"

Abigail hiked faster.

"Maybe that would be enough. Maybe if we showed them the moon rock, then everyone would finally know the amazing stuff you've done. They'd see how smart you are. Maybe they'd leave you alone."

Silence.

"You don't even have to do it. If you give me the moon rock, I'll show them for you." When Abigail didn't answer, I stopped hiking.

"None of it's true, is it, Abigail?" I said. "There is no moon rock."

Abigail pulled her scarves tight and spun away. I tried to keep up, but she was moving too fast.

By the time I got back to camp, she had already removed her snowshoes. I watched her walk up to the front door of the house and tear down the paper Prattle had nailed there. She crumpled it in her fist and tossed it in the fire. Then she retreated to her shed and ducked inside. The latch clicked.

I stared at the boarded-up house. "What are you hiding?" I asked it. "Who is Abigail Jacobs?" But even as I asked those questions, I knew the answers didn't really matter.

Even if I told people that Abigail was an important computer scientist who had worked with famous astronauts and had a moon rock, what difference would it make? No one would believe me. I needed something more than my words.

I thought about Mom and court and how Annie was so brave, the way she told her clients' stories. But Annie didn't use only words. She gathered evidence, too. I knew that was what I needed to prove Abigail was who she claimed to be. Evidence.

I scanned the house knowing there was only one place to find it.

Stay out, stay out, stay out, the house seemed to warn.

But I had other plans.

CHAPTER
12

On Friday morning, Mr. Andrews greeted us. "Welcome, wax figures! Only ten days to showtime!" He cleared his throat and waited for everyone to calm down. "I have made copious notes on your index cards." He strolled down the aisles placing cards on desks. "If you see a lot of red ink, it means you are missing information. You have three days to revise and get these back to me."

When Mr. Andrews's boots stopped at my desk, I looked up. He placed my cards in front of me. *A+* was printed on top. "Great job, Ruby. You worked hard on these." His eyes crinkled in a smile.

Ahmad turned, beaming. "Congratulations, Ruby," he whispered.

Mr. Andrews continued up the aisle. I removed the rubber band and sifted through my cards. There were checks and exclamation points. *Excellent research!* Mr. Andrews had written. I felt my cheeks grow warm, and I felt a lightness I had only felt when I'd gone flying with Abigail. For a moment, I thought that maybe I really could do this. I was so happy right then, even Dakota's icy stare didn't bother me.

●────────●

After school, I followed Ahmad to Rucki's. Mom was working and I wanted to show her my A+ cards.

Inside Rucki's, Mr. Saleem poured coffee for two men huddled at a table. I recognized them as Mayor Eton and Officer Prattle. I heard the rumble of Mom's car starting out back and wondered if she'd taken off when they showed up. I wanted to leave, too, but Mr. Saleem waved me and Ahmad over.

"It's a safety issue," Mayor Eton said as he poured maple syrup into his coffee. He wore a business suit with a bright red tie.

"I went there," Prattle said. "But she wouldn't let me inside. There's nothing I can do without a warrant."

"It was one thing when she stayed inside her—camp or whatever you'd call it," Mayor Eton said. "But lately, folks have been seeing her all over town. My daughter says she's at the town green every morning feeding birds and attracting who knows what kind of vermin. And my wife saw her walking right here on Main Street. Parents have called to report her trespassing at the school. She was standing there, just staring at the kids. There's no telling what she's capable of. It's got to stop."

"It doesn't work like that, Jim. I can't haul an eighty-year-old lady into the station because some people are nervous," Officer Prattle said. "She hasn't done anything wrong."

"I'm the head of the town council. I ran a campaign that promised to clean up Fortin. She's a vagrant and she's making me look like I'm not doing my job." He sipped his coffee. "Plus there's a town ordinance now. I didn't do that myself. The council voted for that."

Mr. Saleem winked and put plates in front of Ahmad and me, but I wasn't hungry anymore.

Prattle sipped his coffee. "You know, my father was

one of the detectives who investigated the accident. You know, with her family."

"What accident?"

"Before your time," Prattle said. "Geez, it must have been at least forty years ago."

"Oh yeah. My wife told me about that," the mayor said. "Didn't they think she had something to do with it?"

"No, it wasn't like that. But you know how rumors start. People wanted answers and the police didn't have any." Prattle snapped his fingers. "It was like her whole family vanished into thin air." He lifted his coffee mug. "Of course, it didn't help that she's always been a loner. For as long as she's lived in Fortin, no one really knows her. I'd almost forgotten about her until she started showing up around town."

The mayor shook his head. "You should have forced your way into that house, Prattle. If she resisted, you'd have a reason to arrest her. Then we wouldn't have to wait." Mayor Eton laughed. "Have you heard that story about how she worked with astronauts?" He snorted. "The stuff people make up!"

Prattle shook his head. "I doubt she knows humans have been to the moon."

I took a sip of water, but my throat only grew tighter.

"One week, Prattle. If you can't get the job done, I'll find someone who will." Eton gulped down the rest of his coffee. "We're doing her a favor."

As the men stood to leave, my heart started beating in my ears. I thought back to the afternoon at school when the kids on the bus were making fun of Abigail, and I had sat there without saying anything. Something inside me couldn't let that happen again. Without even knowing what I was going to do, I felt my body rise up.

Mr. Saleem stepped through the swinging door as Mayor Eton punched his arms into the sleeves of his long black coat.

"We'll take the check, Mr. . . . um . . ."

"Saleem. I am Mohammed Saleem," he said. "It's on the house, gentlemen."

Eton laughed. "I can't get used to John Rucki not being here." He put a dollar on the table and took a step toward the door.

"Mr. Eton," I said.

"Huh?" He turned.

"Umm . . . I heard you talking about Abigail Jacobs and I . . . um . . . I . . ."

Eton gave me a puzzled look that made the prickly pit in my throat grow even bigger. When I didn't say anything, he yanked the door open. The blast of cold air revived me.

"I know Abigail Jacobs. And she's . . . uh . . . she's amazing really, and not only does she take care of, you know, herself, obviously, but she takes care of a lot of animals like birds, deer, rabbits, and . . ."

The mayor didn't step outside, but he let go of the door. The bell dinged as it shut. I felt my face get hot.

"Were you eavesdropping, young lady?" he said.

I tried to swallow, but my throat was too tight.

The mayor put his hands on his hips and stared at me. "That is very rude."

"Wait a minute," Prattle interrupted. "You're the girl who was at her camp the other day."

"I go to school with Dakota," I blurted, unsure why that came out.

Mayor Eton crossed his arms.

"And I can prove Abigail Jacobs is really brilliant," I said. "She did work with astronauts. I can prove it, because they gave her a moon rock."

The mayor started laughing. He nudged Prattle, who

looked as if he was trying to figure out where else he'd seen me.

"You do that." The mayor laughed. "You bring me that moon rock. Ha-ha. We'll put it in a museum for the whole town to see." He pulled the door open again. "And from now on, be a good girl and mind your own business." The bell jingled loudly as the door slammed behind them. I could hear their muffled laughter outside.

My hands were shaking as I sat back down at the counter. I took a sip of water.

Ahmad gripped my shoulder. "You are very brave, my friend," he said.

"Ahmad," I said. "What are you doing tomorrow?"

"It is Saturday. I am working here."

"What about at six a.m.?" I said. "I need your help."

Ahmad pushed up his glasses with his fist. "Of course, Ruby. I will always help you. But I must do morning prayer before the rising of the sun."

"It won't take long. Can you meet me at the bottom of my driveway?"

"At six a.m.?"

I nodded.

"It will be dark."

"Yes," I said. "It will be very dark."

CHAPTER

13

The next morning, the five-thirty alarm woke me with a jolt. My brain tried to trick me into going back to sleep, but I quickly remembered why I had set it for so early.

I had slept in my clothes so I wouldn't make noise getting dressed. In the kitchen, Bob stretched and watched me pack Mom's flashlight and some carrot tops for Scrappy. As I slipped into my boots, he began to whine. I knew that if I didn't take him, he'd bark and wake Mom. I hitched his leash and locked the door behind us.

Outside, the sky was so black it looked as if you could drink it. I felt the darkness seep into my skin. The moon shone like a white disk cut in half. I stood in the road staring at it. "I'll see you on the moon tonight," I whispered.

"Ruby?"

The beam of a flashlight landed on me. I nearly jumped out of my skin. Bob barked.

"What—Is that a dog?" Ahmad said. The light from his flashlight trembled.

Bob pulled loose and pounced on Ahmad.

"Help!" Ahmad yelled.

"Shush, Ahmad! Down, Bob!" I grabbed the end of Bob's leash and pulled on him. Bob rolled onto his back. "Are you okay, Ahmad? I am so sorry!"

Ahmad smoothed his coat.

"This is Bob. He does that when he likes someone. He would never bite you." I glanced at the house to see if a light blinked on from the noise, but it stayed dark. "You can pet him," I whispered.

Ahmad extended a shaking hand. Bob returned the favor with a generous lick. Ahmad giggled.

"Where does this dog sleep?"

"In my room."

"Inside your house?"

"Yeah, of course. Haven't you seen a dog before?"

Ahmad shook his head. "Not like this one."

"We need to go," I said.

"Where are we going, Ruby?"

"We are going to Abigail's camp," I told him.

"Oh, will we feed the birds?"

"Hmmm, something like that."

Ahmad followed me down Specter Hill Road. The breeze kicked up and the wind whistled. With each gust, the skeleton trees rattled their warning: *Stay out, stay out, stay out.* But I wasn't listening anymore.

When we got to the bottom of Abigail's driveway, I shone my flashlight under the pine tree. Scrappy froze in its beam. "Ahmad, this is Scrappy. I feed her every day." I dumped out the vegetables I had brought.

"You have many pets, Ruby."

As Scrappy nibbled on a carrot top, we made our way down Abigail's driveway. When we got to her camp, the fire was completely out. There was no sound from the shed. I looked at my watch: 6:10. I knew I had timed it perfectly. Abigail should have just left for the town green. She wouldn't be back for at least an hour.

I threw my gloves on the ground and opened the seed can. I shone the flashlight inside.

"Will we wait for Mrs. Abigail, Ruby?"

I dug my hand into the seeds, my fingers searching. I swished my arm around until I felt the cold metal. I closed my hand and pulled out the key ring.

"What are those keys for?" Ahmad asked.

I climbed onto the stone step, then glanced toward the driveway. Bob was sniffing around the fire pit.

"What are you doing, Ruby?"

The house was silent now. There were no rattling windows or voices warning me to *stay out*. I felt like the house *wanted* me to come inside. It didn't want to carry its heavy secrets anymore. I knew it as much as I knew the moon rock had to be real.

I started to insert a key, but my ice-cold fingers weren't working right. I fumbled and the keys fell into the snow. I fished them out. *Hurry! Hurry! Hurry!* my brain shouted in time with my pounding heart. I wiped snow off the keys and tried the first one, but it wouldn't go in.

"Ruby?" Ahmad was next to me.

I inserted the second key, and was surprised it fit. But when I tried to turn it, it wouldn't budge. I jiggled it. Nothing.

"Ruby?"

I pulled that key out and tried the last one. It went right in. As I turned it, I heard a *click*. I pushed and the door yawned open. The snow barricade stayed frozen in place. Bob trotted over.

"Come on, Ahmad," I said. "We are going to find that moon rock."

"What?"

"The moon rock. I need you to help me find it."

Ahmad stared at me. "Inside the house of Mrs. Abigail?"

"Well, yeah, where else would it be?"

"Oh, no, Ruby. We have not been invited into Mrs. Abigail's house."

I hadn't expected this. I had thought Ahmad would do everything I said.

"Well, no, but we need to . . . ," I said, hating the whine coming from my voice. "It's our only chance to find out."

"Find out what?" he said.

"To find out if Abigail really worked with astronauts. I need to know if . . . well, if she really did what she says she did. If she has a moon rock inside her house, it will prove it, and I'll be able to stop them from arresting her."

Even in the dark, I could see Ahmad's eyes grow big and round. "You want to find this rock to show the policeman or to show Ruby?"

My mouth fell open in surprise that Ahmad would think that about me. Surprise that he was probably right.

"This is trespass, Ruby. It's stealing," Ahmad said. "It's wrong." He turned and started walking away.

"Ahmad!" I yelled. "I am going inside with or without you." I lifted my foot to step over the snow barricade. Before going in, I glanced back. "Ahmad?" I called.

But Ahmad was gone.

I didn't have time to worry about him. Bob trotted behind me. "Oh no you don't," I said. "Sit, Bob. Stay!" Bob sat.

I stared into the dark shadows of the house. Voices filled my head: *People knew she murdered them. It's her conscience that keeps her outside. My uncle always tells a story about the Bird Lady killing her family. I can never sleep when he tells that story. There are only ghosts in that house.*

Then I took a deep breath and stepped into the darkness.

Inside, I breathed the house's stale air. It smelled as if a whole bunch of winters had been trapped there. My teeth chattered as I shone the flashlight. Thick dust floated in its beam.

I was standing in some kind of workroom or carpentry shop. One wall was filled with tiny holes with metal hooks coming out of them. The hooks held every kind of tool—short saws, fat saws, hammers, a bunch of iron bars—skinny ones, long ones, thick ones. A workbench ran across the length of the wall. It was lined with jars of nails and screws. I placed the keys there so I wouldn't forget them on my way out.

Along the opposite wall, different-sized coats hung in a row. There was a plaid wool coat, a gray sweater, a large yellow raincoat, and a kid's purple jacket.

Below them, women's heels, men's slippers, and pink snow boots waited for feet. A purple scarf had fallen on the floor. I hung it on a hook feeling as though someone might barge in any moment and say, *Hey, what are you doing here?*

I shuddered. *You are here for the moon rock,* I reminded myself. I needed to stay focused. I took two steps up to a door. Someone had painted across it in curly letters: *You are home.*

A herd of scratching claws scurried above me. I sucked in my breath. Squirrels, I thought, or mice. When the noise stopped, I opened the door, and stepped into a large family room. The door shut hard behind me. I jumped. My legs felt weak. *Find the moon rock and get out*, I thought.

I scanned the room. A colorful braided rug covered a dirty warped floor. I stepped around chunks of plaster and dirt. Dust swarmed and floated in drafty gusts, sticking to my clothes and face. I wiped it away with my scarf and sneezed.

A thick iron chandelier dangled crookedly from the ceiling. I was careful not to walk under it, worried it might drop at any second. A stone fireplace took up most of the back. Next to it, a large black watermark stained the wall from floor to ceiling. Floorboards buckled along its edge. A comfy green couch and a rocking chair faced the fireplace.

No moon rocks.

I stepped over pieces of ceiling plaster. A crocheted blanket draped across the couch and spilled onto the floor. I don't know if it was Cecy's voice in my head, but I started folding it. Birdseeds and mouse droppings poured out. I placed it on a cushion and wiped my palms on my jeans.

A book rested facedown on the coffee table: *Tuck Everlasting*. I leafed through its yellowed pages. Some fell loose in my hands. I stuffed them back inside and set the book near a mug with a dark stain.

Next to the couch, puzzle pieces and plaster chips dotted a felt-lined table. The outside edges of the puzzle were finished. The rest of the pieces, sorted by color, sat waiting to be fitted into place. The box cover showed the completed image: the solar system.

I moved in front of the fireplace and lifted a framed picture from the mantel. I wiped off dust to reveal the image of a woman with long hair and a very short skirt. She stood in front of a computer that almost filled the room. Next to her, a stack of papers reached higher than her head. I peered closer and realized it was Abigail. But the photo showed a different Abigail, not just because of her age and styled hair. It was *how* she looked. Her eyes seemed to smile the way they had that day we went flying in the snowstorm. I put the photo down.

There was another picture, of a man with a girl

about my age and a dog that looked like Bob. I couldn't see the girl's face because her long brown hair covered it. They stood by a pond, the girl holding a fish. I immediately liked this girl. I liked the way she held that slippery fish as if it was a treasure.

That's when I saw the newspaper. It was yellow and crinkled in my hands. The headline read: CAR PULLED FROM SIX MILE LAKE. It showed a photograph of a car being hauled out of a large body of water.

FORTIN, VT. Two months after the disappearance of Charlie Jacobs and his daughter, Lillian, divers were able to locate their car, which, it is believed, slid down an embankment during the February nor'easter. Abigail Jacobs, Charlie's wife and Lillian's mother, had initially been identified as a person of interest as the intensive search dragged on with no leads. It appears the heavy snowfall had quickly filled in any tracks the car made when it left the road and slid into the lake. The car's discovery ends months of speculation and panic among Fortin residents anxious to explain the victims' sudden, unexplained disappearance. The deaths have been ruled accidental.

I couldn't take my eyes off the image of the car being dragged out of the lake. My body felt as frozen as the ice spilling from its windows. I placed the paper down. I needed to find something, anything, to get that nightmare scene out of my brain.

I walked over to a wall of framed pictures. The girl with brown hair and dark eyes stared back at me. *Lillian Jacobs, Sixth Grade*, was written across the bottom of a school photo. The girl was in every photo: Lillian with her dog, Lillian reading a book, Lillian feeding the chickadees. I swallowed hard.

I didn't care about the moon rock anymore.

Threads of light began to pour into the room as if a switch had been flicked. They came from tiny holes in the kitchen's boarded-up windows. I walked toward the light. But when I entered the kitchen, a chill ran up my spine. The table was still set from a meal—two cups, two plates, silverware, dried-up bits of food. A yellow flowered apron hung from a cupboard door. A calendar pinned to the wall advertised FORTIN BANK—ALWAYS HERE WHEN YOU NEED US and was open to February 1976. I read the pencil notes scrawled on various days— *Mom in Boston, Lillian—Wax Museum—don't forget the Betamax!, Ginger to Dr. Barrett for shots.*

My hand brushed a bouquet of dead flowers and they disintegrated. A bowl held apples that had shriveled to the size of golf balls. Suddenly, my whole body shuddered as I realized what was really bothering me.

Besides the dead flowers and broken plaster and dust, this could have been our home in Washington, DC, on a day we were late and dashed out—dishes waiting to be cleared, blankets waiting to be folded, books waiting to be read, puzzles waiting to be finished.

Only here, none of that would happen.

Right then, I knew this was the heavy weight that Abigail carried. There had been no murder. No crime. Abigail's secret was that she was trying to keep everything *exactly* the way it was so she could pretend her family was coming back.

People knew she murdered them. It's her conscience that keeps her outside. Stories made up to explain why a person would abandon their home and live in a shed when the truth was much simpler. And sadder.

Stay out.

It was the one thing Abigail had asked of me. The one thing the house had asked.

Stay out.

I had ruined everything.

I moved back to the coffee table. I picked up the book, trying to find the page where its reader had left off. I placed it facedown where it had been. I undid the blanket and let it spill onto the floor. I adjusted the photos on the mantel. Was that how they had been? I wasn't sure anymore.

Stay out! Stay out! Stay out!

It was like the house was waking up. I backed away from the mess I had made, tripping and stumbling into the tool room. I knocked the scarf off its hook, letting it fall to the floor. I tried to open the front door but it was stuck. I panicked, pulling hard on its knob. The door flung open. I ran, tripping over the frozen barricade. The sun was above the horizon now, and its brightness blinded me. The door slammed shut behind me. I sat up, digging my hand into my pocket for the key. But my pocket was empty. As I stood to go back inside, I heard a voice.

CHAPTER
14

"You're here early!" I spun to see Abigail snowshoeing toward me. My mind raced as I practically leaped onto the seed can.

"I—I just got here—I came to—" I took the lid off the can to show her that I was really there to feed the birds. I carried the scoop, spilling with seeds, to the feeders. It didn't help that my hand was shaking. I pulled the wire down and emptied it into the Chock full o'Nuts can. Seeds spilled onto the ground.

"Didn't Bob come with you?" Abigail asked.

I dropped the scoop.

"B-Bob!" I barely choked out his name. "BOB!"

"Calm down, Ruby." She clapped her hands. "Come, Bob!"

I listened for the *clink* of his tags. But the only sound was the rustling of chickadee wings.

"He—He was—" I started. "I—I—"

"You just got here. He couldn't have gone far. Bob!" Abigail called, clapping. "He probably chased a squirrel up a tree and doesn't want to let him down. Come on, put on your snowshoes. We'll find him."

I stood frozen in place.

"What's the matter with you today?" she asked.

My brain shouted, *Move! Go! Find Bob!* But the weight of my crime pressed down on me like a stone.

"I'm going to head out. You catch up when you're ready." Abigail snowshoed into the forest. Her words from when we first met suddenly popped into my head: *Hunters leave traps by the pond.*

I tried to fasten the snowshoes but my fingers wouldn't work. The name LILLIAN JACOBS stared up at me like an accusation. I gave up on the shoes and tried running, but the snow was so deep I ended up crawling onto Abigail's path. That's when I heard a howl. Long and thin and desperate. In a flash, Abigail veered toward the pond.

I followed, half-running, half-falling, my mind thick with worry. "Bob!" I shouted.

"Shush," Abigail said sharply. "If he's trapped, calling his name will make it worse."

That's when I saw my puppy. Lying at the edge of the pond. Covered in blood.

I stifled a sob. "Bob!" I slapped my hands over my mouth. Bob's leg was caught inside the metal jaws of a clamp. He was panting heavily, but managed to smile his goofy-dog smile when he saw me. He started to get up, then yelped and fell down.

The trap was dirty and rusted. Bob licked his paw, but the blood wouldn't stop. It stained his face red and pooled in the snow beneath him.

"Easy, boy, easy." Abigail spoke calmly. She removed her gloves. Bob yelped as she pulled on the jaws of the trap. They didn't budge. Abigail swore.

I stroked Bob's fur and whispered in his ear, "It's okay. You're going to be okay."

Abigail removed one of her scarves. "Get me a stick. We have to stop the bleeding or he'll go into shock."

I found a stick and handed it to Abigail. She had tied her scarf tight around Bob's leg, above the wound. She inserted the stick into the scarf and spun it like a pin-wheel, making it tighter. Bob whimpered.

"We need to find another stick or something to pry open the trap," she said.

I dug a branch out of the snow. Part of it had rotted.

"Not strong enough."

She pulled out a knife and severed a skinny branch. "Hold him so he can't move. Tighter!"

Bob bit at my hand.

She quickly whittled one end and jammed it into the jaw of the clamp. She held one side down with her foot and tried to pry its teeth open, but the branch bent.

"Too green, no good." I watched her scan the woods. Bob seemed to fight for each shallow breath. "I need something stronger. It can't bend."

That's when I remembered the tools I had seen inside the house.

"You have something, Abigail," I whispered.

Abigail looked around frantically. "What? What do you see?"

I bit my lip. If I said it—if I said it out loud—she would know.

"Inside your house."

"What do you mean? The ax is too big. It won't—"

"Not . . . not in the shed. The tools inside your real house." I kept my eyes trained on Bob so I wouldn't see her reaction. "One of those iron poles. That would work."

A sound came from Abigail. Like a balloon had been pricked, the air slowly escaping. The tiniest noise like a mouse might make. And then she was gone.

"Do not cry. Do not cry. Do not cry," I said, holding Bob. Shaking him awake.

I didn't know what to do. If I walked away, Bob would die. If I stayed, Bob would die. I watched his eyes close.

"No! No, Bob!" My nose was running and I felt it freeze on my face. I didn't care.

Don't let me down, Ruby. I'm trusting you to take good care of Bob.

"Bob," I whispered in his ear. "You have to keep your eyes open." I couldn't feel my fingertips anymore, but I tried to open the trap's teeth again. Its rusted jaws would not budge.

Then I took a deep breath and I made the loudest noise I'd ever made—the loudest sound ever made in the history of the world. A sound so loud that astronauts could hear it from space: "PLEASE, ABIGAIL. PLEASE HELP ME!"

I listened to my voice echo across the frozen pond: *ME . . . Me . . . me.* Until the forest sucked up every last vibration. I didn't think I'd ever feel as alone as I did right then.

"I'm here."

I spun around to see Abigail dragging her sled. But instead of wood, it was filled with tools.

I wiped my nose with the back of my hand.

Abigail carried an ax and the long skinny pole I'd seen hanging on the wall. "Turn his body so I can get at that chain." Her voice was sharp and cutting.

Bob winced as I adjusted him.

"Hold him still. I don't care if he cries, he can't move."

Abigail raised the ax and it fell hard, splitting the chain. But the clamp still bit into his foot. Bob yelped as he tried to get up.

"Down, Bob!" Abigail barked.

Bob cowered.

"Hand me the crowbar and stand here on the trap. Put all your weight on it."

I stepped on the bottom half of the trap as well as

I could. Abigail inserted the skinny pole. Heaving and crying, she pried the trap's teeth open just enough. Bob's mangled foot fell out. He tried to stand, but stumbled back.

"Bob!" I hugged his neck.

"He's not out of the woods yet. He's lost a lot of blood." She cleared the tools from the sled. We put our arms under Bob and lifted him onto it.

"This will be difficult. We are going to have to pull together."

We pulled that heavy sled through the snow to Abigail's camp. Up her driveway. Up Specter Hill Road. My shoulders strained and my arms tingled under the weight. Neither one of us spoke a word the entire way.

When we were in front of my house, I let go of the sled's rope and stepped onto the front porch. The door was locked. I pounded. Abigail pivoted on her heel and began walking away.

"Where are you going?" I called.

Abigail lifted a hand and swatted the air like she was swatting away my words. Or me.

"Abigail!"

She slowly turned to face me, her eyes flashing.

"You." Her voice cracked with anger. "You had no right."

I fell back as if she'd hit me.

She narrowed her dark eyes and raised a crooked finger. "Stay off my property," she said. "I don't ever want to see *you* again."

I opened my mouth, "Ab—" I started, but the peach pit was making my throat tight and dry. "Ab—" I tried to cough. Tears lined the rims of my eyes.

The front door burst open. "Ruby? What's happened to Bob?" Mom flew outside in her bathrobe and slippers.

Abigail turned and shuffled away, hunched and small.

"Ruby," Mom said sharply. "I told you to stay away from that lady. What did she do to Bob?"

"Abigail," I whispered after her.

But Abigail was gone.

"We'll talk about this later," Mom said. "We need to get Bob to the vet." We lifted him onto the backseat of the Fiesta. I climbed in after him. The engine roared.

As we drove, Mom's eyes darted between me, Bob, and the road. When we got to the Fortin Animal

Hospital, two men carried Bob in on a stretcher. Mom and I stepped into the waiting room. No one seemed to notice that she was still wearing her bathrobe as she filled out paperwork. I sat on a wooden bench. I was suddenly so tired. But when my eyes drooped shut, all I could see was the dark look on Abigail's face.

Mom slid next to me. "Are you okay?" She wrapped an arm around me. I leaned in to her, breathing her mango-shampoo scent. It seemed like forever since I'd smelled it. I let her warmth seep into me. It seemed like forever since I'd felt it.

The clock on the wall ticked loudly.

Mom kissed the top of my head. "Remember when Dad brought Bob home from the shelter?"

Do not cry. Do not cry. Do not cry.

"You were so excited," she said. "I don't think I've ever seen a smile that big."

I remembered how much I had begged for a dog. But at first Dad shook his head. *Not yet, Ruby*, he had said. *Taking care of a dog is a big responsibility.*

So, when he finally, *finally*, put that furry bundle in my lap, I was so happy I didn't think I would ever stop smiling. But Dad's face stayed serious. He looked me square in the eye. *This is Bob Van Doodle*, he had said.

Don't let me down, Ruby. I'm trusting you to take good care of Bob.

"I wish I could do something to bring your smile back," Mom said, her voice cracking. "I would do anything to see it again. I seem to keep doing the opposite."

I wanted to tell her it was okay, but my tight, dry throat wouldn't let me.

"The trial should be over next week." She took a deep breath. "If going back to DC is what will bring my Ruby back, I'll do it, Ruby. We'll go home." She pressed her moon charm against her lips.

Home, I thought. It's the only thing I've ever wanted.

But no matter how hard I closed my eyes, I could still see Abigail's face, dark and angry. And I could still hear her voice saying she never wanted to see me again.

Do not cry. Do not cry. Do not cry.

• ———— •

Hours passed before a tall, thin lady with silver hair stepped out. "Mrs. Hayes?" she called. The name DR. LISA BARRETT was stitched into her blue scrubs.

We followed the vet into a room. Bob lay on a metal

table, his leg shaved and in a cast. When he saw me, his tail started thumping.

"Oh, Bob!" I buried my face in his neck.

"He's not going for long walks anytime soon," Dr. Barrett said. "But he'll be okay."

"Thank you so much," Mom said.

"My pleasure." Dr. Barrett looked at me. "Really, it was your quick thinking that saved him. Without that tourniquet, he would have bled to death."

But it hadn't been me.

They carried Bob outside and gently slid him onto the backseat, where he could rest his head on my lap. He looked at me with his big brown eyes, sad and confused. I took a deep breath, fighting back the tears. *It's not your fault, Bob. I let this happen.*

When we got to the house, I grabbed a blanket and made a bed for him in front of the woodstove. I filled a bowl with fresh water. Mom warmed last night's beef stew and handed me the dish. "I think Bob earned a treat, don't you?" she said. I knew he must've still been hurting pretty bad, because he only licked at it, then lay back down.

"You've been through a lot today, Ruby. I didn't want to get into it earlier, but what you did was wrong."

She took a deep breath and I knew she was trying not to cry. "I told you not to go down there and you disobeyed me."

I kept my eyes focused on Bob.

Mom knelt next to me. "We need to start talking to each other, Ruby. I know it's my fault and I know you don't always like what I have to say but . . ." She took a deep breath. "We need to talk about Dad."

I felt the tears filling my eyes. I would not blink. I would not speak. I would not cry.

"Ruby—" Mom started.

I shook my head. *No. No. No.*

"Sweetheart. If we don't start talking to each other . . . really talking . . ." She took a deep breath. "You and I, Ruby . . . I'm afraid we're going to disappear, too."

Talk. That was the thing about Mom. She always thought what she had to say would change things. As far as I could tell, talking just made everything worse.

Mom stared at me. When I wouldn't meet her gaze, she stood. "I need to get ready for work. Mr. Saleem is counting on me to have the orders ready for tomorrow." She stepped into her room and closed the door behind her.

I wrapped my arm across Bob's belly, grateful for the rise and fall of each breath.

A little while later Mom came out with her coat on. She stood by the door.

"Stay inside," she said. "We're supposed to get a bad ice storm." The door shut behind her. I heard the Fiesta's engine roar. Soon frozen drizzle pinged against the windows.

I got up and added a log to the woodstove, then snuggled back close to Bob. "You're going to be okay," I whispered. His tail thumped the floor.

As frozen rain pelted the roof, I closed my eyes, wanting to disappear inside the darkness of sleep. Instead, the image I'd seen in the old newspaper—of the car being towed from the icy water—popped into my brain.

I opened my eyes, wondering if Abigail was out in the storm. I wondered if she'd ever come in.

CHAPTER 15

All day Sunday, I tried to talk to Ahmad, but every time I called Rucki's, Mr. Saleem answered and said he was too busy to come to the phone. On Monday morning, I got up extra-early to meet him at the store before he left for school. But when I got to Rucki's, Ahmad was already gone.

When I entered Mr. Andrews's classroom, Ahmad kept his head buried in a book. I sat down and stared at the back of his shirt. Right then I knew how Michael Collins must have felt when Neil Armstrong and Buzz Aldrin left him alone in the *Columbia* while they made their way to the moon—lonely. Bob was barely eating. Annie and Mom were busy preparing for the trial. Abigail never wanted to see me again. I couldn't stand to lose Ahmad, too.

Mr. Andrews stood at the front of the room. "There is exactly one week until the Wax Museum," he said. "Today we are finishing costumes. If you need extra help, you may see Mrs. Puerto in the art room."

I slid out of my seat and moved in front of Ahmad's desk. He wouldn't look up from his book.

"Ahmad," I said.

He didn't budge.

"I'm sorry."

Ahmad turned a page.

I took a deep breath. "I don't know what you want me to do, Ahmad. I'm really sorry."

Ahmad lowered his book. "Prove it," he said.

"What?"

"Prove you are sorry."

"How?"

"You must do something to show how sorry you are."

"Can't you just believe me?"

Ahmad started reading again.

"What do you want me to do?"

He peered over the page. "The Wax Museum. If you are sorry, you will do the Wax Museum with me." Ahmad pushed up his glasses with his fist. "Neil Armstrong and Michael Collins are supposed to be a team."

I shook my head. "You know I can't talk in front of all those people."

Ahmad started reading again.

"That's not fair, Ahmad."

He turned a page.

I started to sit down, then I turned back. "Okay, okay," I said. "I'll do the Wax Museum."

Mr. Andrews walked over. "What's happening here?"

"Mr. Andrews, can Ruby and I go to Mrs. Puerto's room?" Ahmad asked.

"Of course." Mr. Andrews's eyes crinkled.

Ahmad's face broke into a giant grin. I hadn't realized how much I had missed it until that very moment.

"Come on, Michael Collins," he said. "Let's go to the moon!"

In the art room, Mrs. Puerto had rolls of paper and different-sized cardboard boxes and fabric. "Who've we got here?" she asked.

"Astronauts Michael Collins and Neil Armstrong reporting for duty," Ahmad said.

"Let's see what I have." She lifted a big sheet of silvery tinfoil. "This should work."

"Do you have something I can use to make a helmet?" If I was going to do this, I would need more protection than my bangs could offer.

Mrs. Puerto showed us how to form helmets from cardboard and white contact paper. I made mine extra-big with a small visor. I put it on. *Perfect.*

Ahmad turned cardboard boxes into jet packs and oxygen tanks. We decided to wear white clothes underneath. When we had finished, I looked him straight in the eye. "Ahmad," I said. "Thank you."

"You are my friend, Ruby. There is no need to talk—"

"Yes, there is." I took a deep breath. "Ahmad, you have been my friend since I came to Fortin. You were kind to me, no matter how I acted."

"You will always be my friend, Ruby," he said.

And I knew he meant it.

Mom and I spent the rest of that week getting ready to move. I wouldn't let her forget what she'd said that morning at the animal hospital. We would leave for Washington, DC, as soon as the trial was over. We would find a place to rent, hopefully near our old home. Things could finally go back to the way they used to be.

The Sunday night before the trial started, we finished stuffing as many of our things as we could fit into a whole new set of garbage-bag suitcases. Although I'd promised Ahmad I'd do the Wax Museum, I couldn't stop trying to come up with ways to get out of it. I hadn't had the courage to tell him we were moving right after Mom's trial finished, either. Thinking about not seeing Ahmad made my heart feel heavy. I had never had a friend to say goodbye to in any of the other schools I'd been in since DC.

When we had finished packing, Mom stood near the woodstove ironing her dress for court.

"I still don't understand why I can't go to the trial," I said. "You let me go to court before."

"That was different. The trial could go the entire day, maybe two, and I don't want you to hear Chatty's lies. Plus if you're not at school tomorrow, they won't let you do the Wax Museum."

Another reason to go to the trial, I thought. "If it finishes Monday, can we leave right away for DC?"

"After all the work you've done to get ready for the Wax Museum?" Mom shook her head. "And don't expect things to wrap up Monday. Everything moves so slowly in court. Annie says that after the evidence is done, the attorneys do closing arguments and then we have to wait for the jury to deliberate. There's no telling how long that will take."

She let the iron sit a little too long and I could smell burning. "Oh!" She lifted the iron and examined the spot. "It's okay."

"The jury will know you're innocent. They have to."

"Of course. I didn't do anything wrong," Mom said. She pressed the moon charm against her lips.

Later that evening, Mom made chicken cacciatore, which cheered us both up. I told her it was the best thing I'd ever eaten. As I was cleaning up, Mom said, "I'm going to hit the sack early. I'll be gone before you get up." She gave me a kiss on the forehead, then disappeared into her room.

As nervous as we both were, I was relieved it was almost over.

That night, I wore Dad's Air and Space Museum sweatshirt to bed, thinking about how much he loved flying kites at the Washington Monument. *We'll be home before the cherry blossoms are out*, I thought.

●————————●

On Monday morning, I woke to the sound of the Fiesta's roar. It was still dark out.

I padded into the kitchen. Mom must have added wood to the stove before she left. The house felt warm and cozy. There was a basket of blueberry muffins on the table. Next to them sat a small box wrapped in tinfoil. The box was decorated with a red ribbon and a big heart. I had forgotten it was Valentine's Day.

I bit into a blueberry muffin. Still warm. I unwrapped the box. Inside was Mom's crescent moon necklace. I lifted the necklace, watching the silver moon spin. It was engraved: *I love you to the moon and back*. A small piece of paper was tucked into the box: a note. I unfolded it.

To my very brave daughter (aka Michael Collins):

Dad gave me this necklace when he got his first job as a police officer. I had begged him not to take that job. I told him I'd worry every single time he went to work. He told me this necklace would help me to be brave, all I had to do was wear it and think of him.

I asked your father why he needed to be a police officer so badly. He told me something I'll never forget: "Even when you can't see it," he said, "courage can be found when you simply stand up." He told me it was his turn.

Over the last two years, this necklace has helped me get through many challenges. I want you to have it now, Ruby. I hope it will help you be brave at the Wax Museum tonight. Remember, just like the moon in the sky, even when you can't see it, courage is there. All you have to do is stand up. Stay brave, my Ruby Moon, and remember, no matter what happens, I'll see you on the moon tonight.

I love you with all my heart,
Mom

I lifted the necklace. So many times I had begged Mom to let me wear it, but at that moment, it only made my heart feel heavy.

"Mom gave this to me even though she needed it for court," I said to Bob. I took a deep breath and fastened it around my neck. I touched my hand to its moon charm and I stood up.

CHAPTER

16

At school, I still couldn't bring myself to tell Ahmad that we were moving, or that I wasn't sure I'd be able to keep my promise to him that evening.

"Ruby, I will take our costumes to Rucki's," Ahmad had said in Language Arts. "You will meet me there. Neil Armstrong and Michael Collins must go to the Wax Museum together."

I nodded, but my throat felt tight and itchy.

Later, as the afternoon bus made its way up Specter Hill Road, I scanned the woods for a sign of smoke coming from Abigail's camp as I had every day since Bob's accident. But the sky was clear and empty.

I got off the bus and made my way up our driveway hoping to see Mom's Fiesta packed and ready to leave. But the driveway was empty, too.

Mom had said court would go until five and even later if they were near finishing. I hoped that didn't happen. If I was stuck keeping my Wax Museum promise to Ahmad, I needed Mom to be there.

Part of me wanted to believe Abigail would keep her promise, too. She had said that if I did the Wax Museum, she would come.

But when I thought about the dark look on her face, and the mayor's threats, I knew Abigail wasn't going to risk getting arrested to keep a promise to a trespasser like me.

As I unlocked the front door of our house, Bob hobbled up. I hitched his leash and took him outside. Since the accident, he was only able to walk down the driveway and back.

We slowly moved to the edge of Specter Hill Road. Bob sat down and lifted his head to the sky. I smiled. It was as if he was so used to seeing me look for the

moon, he had decided to start doing it, too. I pressed
Mom's moon charm against my lips as I followed Bob's
gaze. Even though it wasn't dark yet, a giant full moon
hovered just above the horizon.

*Did you know that at the next full moon, there is
going to be a Ruby Moon?*

Abigail and I were supposed to watch the lunar
eclipse together. That was the deal we'd made on the
Moon Bench. I thought back to the night we'd watched
last month's full moon rise in the pink-and-purple sky.
For that one moment, I had believed that something as
magical as a Ruby Moon could be real.

I swallowed hard and blinked. It hurt too much to
remember. It hurt to think about everything that had
gone wrong since I broke Abigail's trust.

Right then, I wished with all my might that Mom
would drive into the driveway, the trial over. It would
be so easy to jump into the Fiesta and take off without
ever looking back.

But as the full moon crept higher and higher, the
driveway seemed emptier and the weight on my shoulders heavier. I knew right then that I would never feel
right until I apologized to Abigail.

Back inside the house, I stepped around the garbage-bag suitcases. The place felt as cold and lonely as it had the afternoon Officer Prattle fishtailed his way up our driveway. I grabbed some veggies for Scrappy. I needed to say goodbye to her, too. On my way out, Bob started to follow. "Not yet, Bob," I said. I locked the door behind me.

●————————●

As I made my way down Specter Hill Road, I breathed in the sharp, cold air thinking how I wouldn't be taking this walk again. I felt a pang thinking how much I would miss these woods. They had scared me when I first got to Fortin. But the hikes with Abigail had made me realize they weren't scary once you got used to them. I could breathe in the woods. Somehow, I felt lighter there.

When I got to the frozen gate with its NO TRESPASS-ING sign, I ducked under the pine tree. "Scrappy," I called. Wind rustled the pine needles. I felt a chill and pulled my scarf tight around my face. The wind gusted.

"Scrappy!" I dumped out some lettuce and carrot tops.

But Scrappy didn't come.

I stared down Abigail's driveway. Then my feet started walking.

It had been nine days since Bob got hurt. Nine days since Abigail told me to never come back. My heart raced at the thought of seeing her. I worried she would tell me to leave before I could apologize. I worried that when I apologized anyway, she would slip into her shed and disappear.

Abigail's driveway seemed longer and colder than ever. The wind through its empty trees even lonelier. When I reached her camp, I blinked and spun around, confused. It was as if I'd taken a wrong turn.

The camp was empty. The stones of the fire pit had been removed, the charred wood scattered, the red teapot gone.

I stumbled toward the shed. Its door banged open and shut in the wind. The window frame that had held the shabby quilt was empty. I peered inside. The shed was bare. And then a sinking feeling came over me as I imagined Abigail being handcuffed and dragged away by Officer Prattle and Mayor Eton.

The wind kicked up and the empty feeders bumped together.

I hustled toward the seed can and opened it. The

keys weren't there, and I wondered if they were still sitting on the workbench where I'd left them. The front door I had once entered seemed to frown at me.

My body ached to hear Abigail call the chickadees over. I stared at the shed, feeling as empty and hollow as it looked. I longed to see Abigail's gap-toothed smile.

Without thinking, I opened the seed can and filled the scoop. My feet made their way to each feeder as I emptied the seeds.

"Come back," I whispered as I poured seeds. *"Come back."* My throat ached as I blinked back tears. I studied the house. Its dark window-eyes glared.

What? I wanted to ask it. *What do you want from me?*

But the house stayed silent.

"I'm sorry," I whispered hoarsely.

Prove it, the house seemed to say.

Chick-a-dee, I heard. *Chick-a-dee-dee-dee*. I turned to see a tiny bird land on a seed can. It watched me watching it, then snagged a seed and flew off.

More chickadees landed on the feeders, flying up and down in their crooked, roller-coaster way. I sat on the snowy step, staring at my fingertips where the first chickadee had landed. I thought about how that tiny bird had studied me up and down before deciding to trust me. I remembered how it was brave enough to fly toward me, when the bigger blue jays flew away.

Abigail had made that happen, I thought. And so much more. I knew that her magic was as real as the chickadee's. I had known it all along.

Things I had learned from Abigail suddenly began to fill my head—how to snowshoe through the forest without getting lost, how to fly in the middle of a snowstorm, what needed to happen for a lunar eclipse to become a Ruby Moon—things she'd kept hidden all those years beneath her scarves and sadness.

But Abigail had peeled back her layers when she was with me. Some moments were amazing—like gazing at the stars from the Moon Bench—and some weren't—like when she went to her dark place and disappeared. Not every moment was pretty and happy, but I wouldn't give up a single one of them.

I knew right then that it wasn't an apology the house wanted from me. It was a story. Abigail's story. And I didn't need a moon rock to tell it.

I had to find Abigail. *Mom must be back from court*

by now, I thought. She would know what to do. Annie and Cecy, too.

I took a step, then froze. I needed to leave Abigail a sign, in case she was able to get back here. I needed to let her know that I wouldn't disappear on her again.

The house stared down at me with its bandaged eyes. I lifted Mom's moon charm to my lips, then I slipped the necklace over my head and stepped up to the front door.

If Abigail got back here, she was going to need courage. I hung the necklace on the nail Officer Prattle had left in the door. I watched the silver crescent moon spin in the breeze. *I love you to the moon and back.* Then I started running.

I ran until I got to my driveway. I unlocked the front door and raced inside. I unzipped my backpack, digging through its pockets until I found Mr. Andrews's cork baseball center. I stared at it as if it could talk. Then I started writing.

I wrote and wrote and wrote. I put down everything I knew about Abigail Jacobs. I wrote what it was like to soar through a snowstorm and feel like you could really reach the moon. I sang, *"Come, Josephine, in my flying machine,*" at the top of my lungs as Bob barked along. I scribbled on about the chickadees and what it was like to touch real magic and how every time we were together she made me feel as if I had something really important to say.

I wrote so fast and hard that I almost didn't hear the engine grind its way up the driveway. I ran to the door, anxious to tell Mom about Abigail and how we needed to stop the mayor from locking her up.

But as I yanked the door open, I saw that it wasn't Mom's Fiesta.

"Cecy?" I said when she cut the engine. "What are you doing here?"

Cecy opened her door. She wasn't wearing her sour-milk face. She'd been crying.

"Where's Mom?"

Cecy shook her head. "I'm sorry, Ruby."

The peach pit twisted in my throat. "What?"

"The jury found your mom guilty."

CHAPTER 17

Sometimes people disappear. One minute they're there, then *poof*, like a magic trick, they're gone.

Sometimes you wake one morning, expecting to see your dad at the kitchen table like he is every morning after working the overnight shift, still in his uniform, sipping coffee and hovering over the puzzle section you pieced together the night before. Until one morning you get up and there is only Mom in her bathrobe, opening the door to two police officers who hand her his badge and wedding ring and won't stop saying, *We're sorry, Dahlia. We are so very sorry.*

That night, the night he disappeared, as my dad's

shift was ending, a call came asking an officer to respond to a robbery in progress. He didn't have to go, but he did anyway. That was his job.

My dad was a quiet man. He was brave. But the kid robbing the pizza delivery guy that night didn't care. He took my dad's life for twenty-seven dollars.

That was two years ago.

They say kids don't remember details when really bad stuff happens, but I remember everything from that morning.

I remember the smell of burned toast and the drops of rain coming in the open window. I remember the wet curtains and I remember that no matter how hard I tried to tug the window shut, it wouldn't budge. I remember how Mom tried to fill Dad's empty ring with her finger. I remember how it just kept slipping off.

Maybe it was because I was soaking from the rain or because Mom wouldn't help me close that window, but I cried hard then. I cried and I screamed even though I didn't really understand what had happened or that I'd never get to see my dad again.

I cried and cried until Mom yelled at me to stop. And then I never cried again.

My dad was a quiet man. I liked his quiet. I liked

how we understood each other without words. He always knew which book I wanted to read or what TV show I wanted to watch. No matter how loud the world got, my dad held me. Wordless and safe.

People like quiet, I thought. My dad liked quiet.

Quiet keeps people from disappearing.

Only, it didn't.

CHAPTER

18

Cecy glanced at her watch. *"It's four o'clock now.* Why don't I drop you off at Rucki's? You need to be at the school at five to get ready for the Wax Museum, right?"

I stared at Cecy. Did she really think I was still going?

She stepped into Mom's room and came out with a handful of clothes. She found an empty bag and put them in it.

"What are you doing?" I asked.

"Your mom wanted me to grab some things before they bring her to the women's prison."

"Mom's still at the courthouse?"

Cecy opened the door. "If they haven't taken her yet."

"I want to see her."

"I'm sorry, Ruby. You can't."

"Please, Cecy. I have to."

●────────────●

Sitting next to Cecy on a bench outside the courtroom, I felt the scratchy peach pit rise and lower inside my throat. But no matter how hard I swallowed, it wouldn't go away.

Annie walked up to us. "Well, I've been meeting with the judge in chambers," she said. "This isn't over yet."

"What do you mean?" Cecy said. "The jury found Dahlia guilty and the judge sentenced her to twenty days in jail."

I shivered when I heard the sentence. Even though it could have been a year, even one day was too much.

"Yes," Annie said. "But you know me. I've got a couple tricks up my sleeve."

I wanted to ask what tricks she could possibly have left, but the peach pit wouldn't let me.

"Ruby was hoping she could see her mom," Cecy said.

Annie shook her head. "I'm sorry, Ruby. They don't let the public into the lockup."

I strained my voice, willing it to speak. "Please, Annie," I whispered.

Annie bit her lip. "Let me see what I can do."

•————•

A court officer brought me into a tiny room, where I sat on a hard metal stool. The space was so small, Cecy couldn't fit in there with me. The room was separated from another room on the lockup side by a window that had metal wire running through it. Even with the glass barrier, I could hear shouting and banging going on back there.

Another officer brought my mom into the room on the lockup side. Chains clanged with each step. She was still wearing the dress she went to court in, but someone had taken her shoes and jewelry. Now her hands were cuffed. She sat on a metal stool opposite me. Her eyes were red and swollen.

"Oh, Ruby," she said. "I'm—"

Seeing Mom like that made the peach pit in my throat grow and grow and grow. I tried to swallow it back, but instead it exploded into a million tears, erupting and streaming down my face like lava from a volcano. For the first time in two years I cried. Not just regular tears, but big, heaving, hiccupping, sloppy sobs.

I cried for my mom, chained like an animal. Punished for speaking up. I cried for myself, abandoned again. And finally, finally, I cried for my dad, and how I missed him so much it hurt my insides every single day.

Tears streamed down my face. I opened my mouth to talk, but only choking sounds came out. I cried so hard my whole body shook.

Mom pressed her shackled hands together against the window. "*Shhh*, Ruby. I'm sorry. I'm so sorry."

I lifted my hands against the glass so it almost looked like we were touching.

An officer peered in, probably checking to see what all the noise was about, but when he saw us, he pursed his lips and walked away.

We sat there, Mom and me, crying two years of sadness, until there were no tears left. I tried to talk again, but instead my whole body hiccupped.

Mom's head fell forward. "I've ruined everything."

I peered at her through blurry eyes.

"You were right, Ruby." She shook her head. "Speaking up didn't change anything. It just got me in more trouble."

My skin prickled.

"Keep your head down. Keep your mouth shut. That's how it's going to be from now on," she said. Tears rolled down her cheeks.

"But you couldn't let them get away with it," I said. "You had to tell the truth."

She lowered her cuffed hands. "As soon as this is over we'll leave Fortin. I'll be a different person, Ruby. We'll pretend none of this ever happened."

I stared at her. It was what I had wanted her to say ever since we got to Vermont. But it didn't make me feel the way I'd thought it would.

Mom sniffled. "I miss Dad so much. Moving to all those cities where we had gone on vacation—I thought that would take away some of the hurt. But it didn't." She shook her head. "And now this. I should have kept my big mouth shut."

"You had to tell your side of the story."

Mom wiped her face with her shoulder. "Didn't do us much good, did it?"

But as I sat there in that tiny room, I knew that it had.

"The Wax Museum is tonight," she said.

I bit my lip.

"You don't have to do it, Ruby. You don't have to do anything you don't want to." She lifted her chin. "But you know what?" She smiled. "You would have made a great Michael Collins."

But I'm not like Michael Collins, I thought. *You are. Michael Collins is brave.*

"You'll have to stay at Cecy's while I'm . . ." Her words trailed off.

The court officer opened the door on Mom's side. "They need you back in court, ma'am."

I waited for Mom to say something else. Anything else. But her words seemed to have dried up with her tears.

As the officer led her away, her gaze fell to the floor and her bangs covered her face.

After Mom left, I sat there, breathing uneven breaths.

It was wrong. Everything. Not just Mom going to jail but the way they lied and got away with it.

"My mom stood up," I said to no one. "She wins." Then I wiped my face with the back of my sleeve and stepped outside.

Cecy was waiting. "You are a wet, hot mess," she said as she handed me a tissue.

I blew my nose. "Cecy," I said.

"Mmmm-hmmm?"

"Are you going home now?"

"Annie just went back into court. She wants to talk to me when she's done."

I started to reach for Mom's necklace, then remembered I'd left it at Abigail's. "Can you take me to Rucki's first? Ahmad has my stuff for the Wax Museum."

Cecy looked at her watch. "If we hurry, I think we have time."

●———————————●

Cecy dropped me at Rucki's, anxious to get back to the courthouse.

"You'll be at the Wax Museum when it starts at six, right, Cecy?" I asked.

The clock on her car read five o'clock. "I'll do my best."

The bell rang as I opened the door to Rucki's. Ahmad emerged from the back wearing his Neil Armstrong space suit. He handed me my index cards and costume. "Hello, Michael Collins! Are you ready for the moon?"

I hiccupped loudly.

"Are you okay, Ruby?" Ahmad asked.

"Oh, good, Ruby, you are here!" Mr. Saleem said. "We are already late." He limped to the window and flipped the sign to CLOSED.

"Can I use your bathroom?" I whispered.

Mr. Saleem looked at his watch.

"Quickly, Ruby," Ahmad called as I dashed off.

In the bathroom, I stared at my image in the mirror. My face looked pale and thin. My hair, a knotty mess. There were dark circles under my eyes.

I can't do this, I thought. *I can't speak in front of all those strangers. I can't even speak in front of my sixth-grade class.* I stared at the index cards in my hand. The smiley face next to where Mr. Andrews had written *Excellent research!* stared back.

Everyone I knew had left me. First Dad, then Abigail, and now Mom. Even Cecy wouldn't be there.

"Ruby, we must hurry!" Ahmad called.

Without looking back, I tossed the index cards in the garbage. I would not need them tonight.

● —————— ●

Backstage, behind the closed curtain, a nervous buzzing surrounded me. I was almost excited until I remembered I wasn't part of it. I was there but not there. I tried to look invisible as Mr. Andrews approached.

"Great costume, Ruby! Let's see it with the helmet on."

I put the giant cardboard helmet on my head. Although it made it harder to breathe, it was easier to hide.

"Awesome! I am so proud of you, Ruby. I know it hasn't been easy, but I can't wait to hear your performance tonight. The crowd is going to love Michael Collins but they are going to love Ruby Hayes even more!"

I turned away.

"Oh wait, I almost forgot." Mr. Andrews handed

me a padded envelope. "Someone left this here for you." The envelope read: *URGENT for Ruby Moon Hayes.*

"Help! Mr. Andrews! My costume isn't staying together!"

"Hold on, Sophia, I'll be right there." Mr. Andrews placed the package in my hand and strode off.

I removed my helmet and opened the envelope. A hard object fell into my palm. As I turned it over, I saw that it was a small gray rock encased in glass. The rock looked like something you'd find in someone's driveway, except attached to the bottom of the glass was a gold plaque. It read:

THIS FRAGMENT OF ROCK WAS GATHERED AT THE SEA OF TRANQUILITY OF THE MOON. IT IS GIVEN TO ABIGAIL JACOBS IN GREAT APPRECIATION OF HER CONTRIBUTION TO THE SPACE PROGRAM. FROM THE ASTRONAUTS OF APOLLO 11—NEIL ARMSTRONG, BUZZ ALDRIN, MICHAEL COLLINS

Right then, a warmth spread through my body. I scrambled to the edge of the stage and peeked around the curtain. In the auditorium, people greeted each other and took their seats. I scanned the audience, but there was no Abigail.

I clenched the rock in my fist, trying to wrap my brain around the fact that I was actually holding a piece of the moon. The real moon.

"Places, people!" Mr. Andrews bellowed. The lights flashed and went dark as everyone got into the positions they would hold until the spotlight hit them. The dull roar of the audience filled my ears.

Bright red letters flashed EXIT over the outside door. They pulled me toward them like a moth toward a light. I pushed the door open a crack, feeling the clear, cold February night on my face. *This is it*, I thought. *I can walk away right now.*

But something made me glance back at the stage, where my classmates stood frozen in their poses. In the shadow of the curtain, they really did look like a museum of wax statues.

I turned toward the frozen air. That's when I saw the moon—giant and glowing. The same moon my dad and I had searched for each night. The same moon Abigail and I had gazed at from the Moon Bench.

I tried to remember what Abigail had told me would happen next. The moon would disappear in the shadow of Earth and when it reappeared, it would be glowing and red. It would be a Ruby Moon.

Suddenly, a hand was on my shoulder. "Ruby, come on." Ahmad stood beside me. He placed the helmet on my head. Then he took my hand and led me toward the stage.

"I—I can't, Ahmad." But the helmet stifled my words. "Ahmad, stop, wait," I shouted. But Ahmad kept pulling me through the wax figures to the spot marked MICHAEL COLLINS.

Ahmad took his own place as the curtain slowly opened. I swallowed hard.

"Remember," Mr. Andrews whispered, "speak naturally, but have your index cards handy in case you get stuck."

I looked at my hands. Empty except for the moon rock.

As the curtain lifted, the audience went crazy with applause. I found Mr. Saleem right away and he gave me a little wave. Officer Prattle stood by the entrance. Dakota's dad, Mayor Eton, sat in the front row. No matter how hard I searched, there was no Cecy. No Abigail.

Cameras flashed. Parents and grandparents waved

at their kids. But the wax figures stayed in position, still as statues.

A microphone lowered from the ceiling. The crowd became silent.

Mr. Andrews stepped beneath it. "Welcome, everyone, to the Sixth-Grade Wax Museum!" he said. The crowd erupted all over again with applause and whistling.

"Tonight we will travel through space and time to the far corners of the universe to meet the most fascinating people the world has known. I ask that you hold your applause until the end." Mr. Andrews went backstage, where he'd control the spotlight. As he walked past me he said, "Relax, Ruby. I'm going to have you go last."

The lights dimmed. The spotlight hit Ahmad.

"My name is Neil Armstrong, and I am the first man to walk on the moon." It was hard to hear Ahmad over the buzzing in my ears. But from the corner of my visor I watched him wave his arms, his voice raising and lowering. The audience laughed in appreciation. I suddenly felt so proud of my friend, who only two years ago couldn't speak English.

Ahmad finished and the spotlight moved on to Dakota. "My name is Diana, Princess of Wales . . ."

I hugged myself and scanned the audience. But my arms dropped when I saw the shapeless figure standing alone in the corner. She wore a patched wool coat and was wrapped in so many scarves you couldn't see her face, but I'd know her anywhere. Abigail had come.

"My name is Sonia Sotomayor and I am the first Hispanic and third woman appointed to the United States Supreme Court . . . ," I heard Melanie begin. Eventually the spotlight moved to Dr. Martin Luther King Jr. and Bethany Hamilton.

Abigail raised a hand in a small wave and a warm feeling washed over me like a sunbeam. I exhaled all the air that I had been holding in my lungs.

As the spotlight jumped around the stage, my heart began to pound so hard I thought my ribs might crack. I turned my head, finding the bright red flashing EXIT sign. It would take only three steps to get offstage.

But as I looked into the audience, I saw that Abigail had moved closer. She had removed a layer of scarves and stood at the back of the center aisle.

Right then, a vision of Scrappy popped into my head.

Eyes wide but seeing nothing. And I knew that was how Abigail must be feeling as she crept up the aisle. But when she removed her coat and continued forward, she seemed to stand a little taller, just as she had that day in the middle of the snowstorm. Tall as a forest tree.

Heads turned and neighbors leaned in to each other, whispering, as they became aware of her. But Abigail kept moving toward the stage. Toward me. I watched her remove more scarves. Peeling them away like baseball yarn.

Mayor Eton motioned to Officer Prattle, who slipped behind her.

I watched Officer Prattle's hand shoot out to grab Abigail's arm, but she stayed out of his reach, her eyes focused on me.

Even when you can't see it, courage can be found when you simply stand up.

That's what Dad had said. It was the reason Mom went to trial even though she had everything to lose. Maybe it was the one thing she couldn't stand to lose—the courage to tell her story. Besides her family, that was the biggest thing Abigail had lost.

The problem comes when you don't speak at all. Then you're letting someone else tell your story.

Maybe it was because she was too lost or too broken. Maybe it was because she was too scared to try—but all that empty space around Abigail had gotten filled with gossip and lies, people pretending to explain something that made no sense. *What makes someone as magical as Abigail Jacobs disappear?*

But there was more to Abigail's story than anyone in town knew—certainly not Dakota or the mayor. Not Mom or Cecy or Mr. Saleem. I was the only person who knew how amazing Abigail Jacobs really was.

Mayor Eton popped out of his seat, his eyebrows knit in an angry frown. He inched toward Abigail, waving at Officer Prattle, who was still out of reach of her.

That's when the spotlight hit me.

The brightness blinded me. I opened my mouth but no sound came out. I felt inside my pocket for the index cards, but my hand dropped when I remembered they were in the garbage at Rucki's.

The audience whispered and shifted in their seats. I heard Mr. Andrews's voice offstage: "Go, Michael Collins! GO!"

I stood there. Eyes wide, seeing nothing. I clenched my hands. That's when I felt the moon rock. Tight in my fist. It looked like an ordinary rock but it meant so much more.

You're going to have to find your own Ruby-magic.

"I—um—I—" I began. But the helmet muffled my words.

I felt a hand on my shoulder and Ahmad was by my side, smiling his goofy smile. He lifted the helmet off my head.

I squinted into the audience. "My . . . um . . . my name . . ."

Mayor Eton was next to Abigail now, but when I began speaking, he stopped and stared. Officer Prattle's hand fell back by his side. People yelled at them to sit down.

My throat felt tight and dry. I coughed. My heart hammered in my chest.

Then Abigail smiled her gap-toothed smile, and I knew what I had to do.

"My name," I said. "My name is Abigail Jacobs."

CHAPTER
19

I closed my eyes. All the things I had written down earlier about Abigail swirled in my head like snowflakes in a blizzard. I opened my mouth, then closed it, my mind going crazy trying to figure out how to start. Then, one word flashed across my brain. My eyes popped open.

"Brave," I said.

People shifted in their seats. A man coughed.

"My name is Abigail Jacobs and I'm brave."

I watched the audience watch me. Every bone in my body screamed, *Run! Go! Hide!* But I didn't move.

"Most of you think you know me. You think I'm crazy

and scary because I don't act the way other people do. I live in the woods and I spend more time talking to birds than people."

A nervous titter skipped across the room. I gripped the moon rock, smooth and cold. *My own Ruby-magic.*

"So I'm here to tell you the truth." I took a deep breath. "I am a brilliant computer programmer who helped bring the Apollo 11 astronauts to the moon and home again."

As if my words were a frozen gust waking everyone up, people shifted in their seats, their hard metal chairs scraping the floor. Foreheads wrinkled. A man in the front row laughed as if I'd told a joke. People hushed him. Then silence.

I glanced at Abigail, worried she'd retreat. Worried the truth would chase her into the dark winter waiting outside. But instead, we locked eyes, staring so hard that the entire auditorium melted away. Frowning faces and crossed arms disappeared until it felt like it was only the two of us. My eyes asked her a silent question. Abigail nodded and I knew she was giving me permission to share the rest of her story. With a shaking fist I held up the moon rock for everyone to see.

Arms unfolded. Necks craned. A woman in the front row stood. People hissed at her to sit.

"I'm holding a piece of the moon. The real moon. Brought to Earth by the Apollo 11 astronauts. It was given to me by Neil Armstrong, Buzz Aldrin, and Michael Collins to thank me for my work."

Everyone stared at the moon rock. They stared at me. I felt sweat trickle down the back of my neck. I gulped.

"I was one of the first women computer programmers in the country. My code . . . the code that I wrote with the rest of my team, instructed the *Eagle* to land on the moon." I nodded. "And later to take off again to rendezvous with Michael Collins in the *Columbia*."

I searched the audience for a reaction, but every eye was glued to the moon rock as though I'd reached into the sky and pulled it down myself.

"B-but that's only part of my story. Some of you remember the accident." I bit my bottom lip to stop its quiver. "There was so much pain. It was a lot easier to disappear than deal with it." I stared at my feet. "And maybe it was easier for you, too . . . to make up stories and lies because . . . well, sometimes facing the truth is a lot harder . . . Sometimes you have to be really brave to do that."

I sucked in a deep breath. "Even though you haven't seen me in a long time, it doesn't mean I haven't been here. It doesn't mean I haven't been trying to find my own way to be brave.

"But now I know. Bravery can be different things to different people." I turned toward Ahmad. "Being brave can mean coming to a new school when you don't know the language." I looked at Melanie. "Being brave can be going into the cafeteria alone and hoping to find a friend." I blinked. "Being brave can be something as big as flying to the far side of the moon . . . or something as small as standing up." I stared at Abigail. "And telling the truth."

I took another deep breath. "I have been many things in my life. A wife, a mother, a scientist, a friend . . . but most importantly"—I raised my chin, stretching myself as tall as a forest tree—"I am brave." I nodded at the audience. "My name is Abigail Jacobs, and now you know my story."

The auditorium was silent as the spotlight stayed on me. I couldn't believe everything that had come out of my mouth. I took a step back into the darkness and suddenly felt so tired.

That's when the applause began. A few claps at first. And then more and more until it became as loud as thunder. I watched Mr. Saleem stand and face Abigail, who was backing down the aisle. She froze. Others followed, standing and clapping. Someone whistled. The applause grew and grew until the whole audience was cheering. I smiled a real smile then. A smile that was bigger than the moon itself. I smiled because Fortin was giving the Bird Lady a standing ovation.

●————————●

Everything started to go a little crazy then. Parents rushed the stage, kids crowded around me, trying to see the moon rock. Ahmad grabbed my shoulders and guided me away. "You were most awesome, my friend."

Kids started jumping off the stage, scrambling to have their pictures taken in their costumes. I scanned the crowd for Abigail, but in the chaos, I'd lost her.

I followed Ahmad toward Mr. Saleem, who took both

of my hands in his. "Ruby, you—how you say—steal the show!"

People pushed and shoved. I spun, searching. But Abigail was nowhere in sight.

"Looking for something?" a voice said. And there was Abigail, eyes brimming with tears. I dropped my helmet and hugged her tight.

"I thought I'd never see you again!" I held out the moon rock. "I am so sorry."

Abigail closed my fingers around it. "That's yours. It's a gift," she said. "Ruby, I'm the one who's sorry. After I left you, I did a lot of thinking. You—making me go into the house—it's what I needed. You are what I needed, Ruby Moon."

"You went in on your own. You did it to save Bob," I said.

"Well, I sure needed a good shove." She looked me square in the eye. "Ruby, I need to tell you that my husband, Charlie, he's gone." Her voice trembled. "My Lillian is gone. They—they are never coming home. I can't lose you, too, Ruby. I can't."

"But what happened to your camp?"

Abigail clutched the crescent moon necklace

sparkling around her neck. "I went . . . Well, what I want to . . ." She nodded. "I want to try to move back inside, Ruby." She took a deep breath. "I think it's time for me to go home."

I hugged her again, because I knew how hard that would be, but I also knew how important it was to find your true forever home.

We stayed like that, silent and safe inside the commotion of the Wax Museum. I breathed in her scent of black licorice and felt only lightness.

"Ruby! Ruby!" Cecy was pushing through the crowd waving her hands in the air. "I'm here. I saw the whole thing!"

But what I saw behind her made me completely lose it. Looking a little dazed and pale, Mom wove through the crowd trying to keep up, her eyes big and round, Annie right behind her.

"Mom! Mom! You're here! How did you get here?"

"Oh, Ruby," Mom said. And she held my face in her hands like she hadn't seen me in a million years. "Your smile, Ruby." She hugged me tight.

"I told you I had a few tricks up my sleeve," Annie said. "It's called an appeal bond. Cecy posted it. The judge agreed to let Dahlia out while I challenge the verdict. Turns out, there's been some witness intimidation going on. This thing's not over yet."

"You mean Mom might not have to go to jail?"

"I didn't say that. We'll see what happens, but some of the ladies at the diner who were too scared to testify . . . well, when they heard how your mom stood up to Chatty, they were inspired to speak up. They collected notarized statements. Before court adjourned, I made a motion to reopen the case based on newly discovered evidence. The judge is allowing your mom to stay free until he reviews that."

"Thank you, Annie," I said. "Thank you for everything."

"Don't forget our secret." She winked at me. "Your speech was something else. Sounds to me like you found your Ruby-magic."

I smiled, gripping the moon rock in my fist. Mom's gaze moved beyond me. Her eyes got big and I knew who she'd seen.

"Mom, I want you to meet my friend Abigail Jacobs," I said.

Mom extended her hand. "I'm happy to finally meet you, Mrs. Jacobs." And then Mom did something crazy.

She reached out and gathered Abigail in a giant hug. I watched Abigail's eyes brim with tears and I realized that sometimes when people cry, it's out of joy, not sadness, and there's no way to know that until you know the whole story.

I remembered how there was a social worker in Annie's office and how she helped clients with lots of different problems. "Annie," I said. "This is my friend Abigail Jacobs."

Annie took her hand. "It's a pleasure, Mrs. Jacobs."

"Abigail and I need your help, Annie. We need to get her house fixed up so she can live in it again."

Abigail stared at her boots. "It's more than the house that needs help, I'm afraid."

"Help is my specialty." Annie winked at me. "There are a lot of resources I can set you up with. Can I introduce you to some people?"

Abigail nodded.

"I can help, too," I said. But I felt a pang, knowing we were packed and would leave soon for DC.

Right then, Melanie, still in her black justice robe, walked past me, carrying her sister. I almost didn't recognize her without her orange coat. Before I could say anything, she disappeared into the crowd.

"Mom," I said. "I'll be right back. I need to talk to someone."

Mom nodded. "Ahmad, I missed your presentation. Tell me about Neil Armstrong."

I scanned the audience until I found Melanie moving against the sea of people.

"Melanie!" I called. But she didn't turn around.

I pushed through the crowd until I caught her eye. I waved my hands.

She spun around to see who I was waving at.

I grabbed the sleeve of her robe. "Melanie!" I laughed. "I'm waving at you!"

"Astronaut." Melanie's little sister pointed at my costume.

Melanie put her down, and I gently placed my helmet on her head. It wobbled to the side. She giggled and shot her arms out. "I can fly!"

"My name is Ruby, by the way," I said, grinning. "I know you saw me in court and, well, obviously I saw you. I wanted you to know that I was embarrassed and that's why I ignored you before. I'm sorry."

She looked at me, confused.

I shrugged. "Anyway, if you ever want to talk about

stuff, I can be a good listener. Ahmad and I usually eat lunch in Mr. Andrews's room. Do you want to join us tomorrow?"

Melanie's face spread into a large grin. She nodded.

"Great!" I said, and I don't know if she thought I was crazy right then, but I reached out and hugged her. "You and me," I said, "I hope we can be good friends."

———•———•———

Later, when it was only Mom, Mr. Saleem, Cecy, Ahmad, Abigail, and me left in the auditorium, Mr. Andrews walked over.

"I had no idea we had a living legend in our midst." He grinned at Abigail. "You know, I was talking to our Science teacher, Mrs. Connelly, and we were wondering if you would speak at a school assembly. We would love to hear more about the work you did for Apollo 11."

Abigail turned toward me. "Maybe someday," she said. "Maybe if I have a friend by my side."

The corners of Mr. Andrews's eyes crinkled. "Ruby, that was quite a speech you gave. I'm really proud of you."

"Thanks for making me do it," I said.

"That was all you," he said. "But I hear you're leaving us."

Ahmad was suddenly by my side. "What is this? You are going somewhere, Ruby?" I thought I heard his voice catch.

Abigail stopped talking to Annie. "What's this?" she said.

Mom turned to face me.

Everyone was waiting for me to say something, but right then I was thinking about Abigail's house. I was thinking about how she wouldn't go inside because it was easier to pretend her family was coming home than accept the truth. Just like it was easier for me to pretend everything would go back to the way it was if we moved back to Washington, DC.

I didn't want to pretend anymore.

My eyes met Mom's. "We don't know what we're doing yet," I said. "Mom and I have to figure that out."

Mom put her arm around me. "Together," she said.

We followed Mr. Andrews outside. He locked the auditorium behind us. As we made our way toward Mom's car, Abigail grabbed my arm and pointed at the sky. There, floating above us like a magic trick, was the full moon in all its glory, bravely shining on us. But right then, it glowed red. Bright red. Like a Valentine heart or a rocket ship. Red like a ruby.

"I heard there was going to be a lunar eclipse tonight!" Mr. Andrews said. "That is truly spectacular!"

"Oh, Ruby, it's just like the night you were born," Mom said.

"I'll see you on the moon tonight," I said.

Mom smiled and I knew she was trying not to cry. "We're going to be okay, Ruby. You and me." She squeezed my shoulder. "My forever home is wherever you are, Ruby Moon."

Mr. Saleem pointed at the bright red moon. "It is a Ruby in the Sky!" he said.

"Unpredictable, rare, and spectacular," Abigail said. "Like our Ruby."

CHAPTER 20

Sometimes people disappear. One minute they're there, then *poof*, like a magic trick, they're gone.

On that April afternoon, when Annie called to say the charges against Mom had been dismissed, and Mom and I took Bob for his first big walk since his accident, that is what I thought about. People disappearing.

As we made our way down Specter Hill Road, I thought about how I'd never be able to stop bad stuff from happening. The only power I had was choosing what to do if it did. I could choose to disappear. Or I could choose to stand up.

When we reached the NO TRESPASSING sign, I showed Mom the pine tree where I'd last seen Scrappy. Her nest was still empty, but the veggies were gone, and I knew in my heart that she'd left the safety of her pine tree to share her lettuce and carrot tops with some new bunnies.

Mom stared down Abigail's driveway. I linked arms with her and gave her a tug. When we reached the place where her campfire had been, I stopped to stare at the house. Its paint was still faded and chipped, but Ahmad and Mr. Saleem had removed the boards from its windows and replaced the broken panes. Now they were clean and bright, letting the spring sunshine inside. Lighting the darkness.

The warm breeze blew the recycled feeders together like wind chimes and I wondered if the chickadees were still around or if they had moved on as they did in spring.

I walked over to the seed can and opened it. I filled the scoop and brought it to where Mom stood.

"Hold out your hands, Mom. It's your turn to hand-feed the chickadees," I said.

"Oh—I don't know, Ruby. I can't—"

"I'll show you. Please. Put your hands together." I poured the seeds into them.

Bob and I moved near the can.

"Stand still, like a statue," I whispered.

Mom smiled and suddenly I felt so light, watching her. I felt like a bird released from a cage it had been stuck in for a long time—eager to go fly and be free.

And that feeling—being free to do whatever I wanted and not knowing what was next . . . well, that was scary, too, and it hit me that maybe the scary part was what made the rest of it worthwhile. I knew then that I would never go back inside that cage even if it meant I'd have to be brave over and over and over again.

Right then, a chickadee flew toward my mom. Its flight wasn't smooth, but all crazy, up and down, like the way I felt when I had to talk sometimes. I watched it land squarely on her fingertips and take a seed in its beak.

I touched my own fingertips, remembering the feeling of being close to something so wild, and I thought how brave that little bird was to take a chance on Mom—to take a chance on me.

The bird flew away as suddenly as it had come and Mom's face broke into a giant smile. I heard a tapping.

Abigail was at the window, waving and smiling and holding up her red teapot. She motioned for us to come inside.

I looked at Mom. She was scanning the darkening sky and I knew what she was looking for. But the sky was clear and empty.

"You know it's there, even though we can't see it," I said as her eyes met mine.

"I know, Ruby Moon," she said. "I know."

Bob barked and Mom let the seeds fall onto the ground.

"Something for the squirrels," I said.

Mom put her arm around me and as we stepped inside to have tea with Abigail, I knew we had finally found our way home.

AUTHOR'S NOTE ON FICTIONAL LUNAR ECLIPSES IN THIS STORY

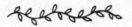

As Abigail Jacobs said, *Ruby moons are very real. But rare. They only happen during a total lunar eclipse.*

Ruby moons—or blood moons, as they are often called—are very real. However, the one that takes place in Ruby's story is fictional. There has not been a total lunar eclipse on Valentine's Day in recent history.

Nevertheless, Ruby moons do happen and are even more magical to experience in person. To learn more about lunar eclipses, and to find out when the next total lunar eclipse will be visible from where you live, please check out the following resources:

The NASA Eclipse website includes a catalog of lunar eclipses through 2100:

eclipse.gsfc.nasa.gov/LEcat5/LE2001-2100.html.

A great source for learning about lunar eclipses is maintained by Fred Espenak, aka Mr. Eclipse, a retired astrophysicist from NASA's Goddard Space Flight Center. It can be found at:

mreclipse.com/Special/LEprimer.html.

A wonderfully technical book filled with diagrams, maps, and data, also by Espenak, is: *Thousand Year Canon of Lunar Eclipses 1501 to 2500*, Portal, AZ: Astropixels, 2014.

Finally, if you wish to learn more about astronaut Michael Collins, please check out his autobiography:

- *Flying to the Moon: An Astronaut's Story*, New York: Farrar, Straus and Giroux, 1994.

Other books about Michael Collins include:

- *The Man Who Went to the Far Side of the Moon: The Story of Apollo 11 Astronaut Michael Collins*, by Bea Uusma Schyffert, San Francisco: Chronicle Books, 2003.

- *The Far Side of the Moon: The Story of Apollo 11's Third Man*, by Alex Irvine, illustrated by Ben Bishop, Thomaston, ME: Tilbury House, 2017.

Enjoy watching the next lunar eclipse—I look forward to seeing you there!

ACKNOWLEDGMENTS

While writing Ruby in the Sky, *I found myself on a* journey that turned out to be as bumpy and steep as Ruby's trip to Vermont. I could not—and definitely would not have wanted to—take this crazy ride alone. I'd like to thank everyone who supported me along the way.

First of all, special thanks to:

- Janine O'Malley, Melissa Warten, and the whole team at Farrar Straus Giroux Books for Young Readers. Thank you for loving Ruby as much as I do.

- My agent, Stacey Glick, of Dystel, Goderich and Bourret. Thank you for hearing Ruby loud and clear and wanting to share her strong voice with the world.

One of the most phenomenal aspects of the world of children's literature is the unwaveringly selfless manner in which this community shares its time and talent. Thank you to:

- Patricia Reilly Giff—as I sat in your Sunday morning classes, I often pinched myself to make sure I wasn't dreaming . . . I'm still not so sure. Thank you for sharing your timeless experience and infinite talent. Your students remain forever grateful.

- Stephen Roxburgh and Carolyn Coman—a couple who have been known to brave hurricanes in order to help aspiring authors. Abigail thanks you for getting her out of the chicken coop. I thank you for teaching me how to write a novel.

- My Pitch Wars mentors, Laura Shovan and Tricia Clasen, for helping me hear Ruby's voice, understand her truth, and tell her story in the way she wanted all along. Team TLC rocks! Thank you to Brenda Drake for creating Pitch Wars. I hope that one day I can give back to this amazing community a fraction of what you all have given to me.

- Bette Anne Rieth—you are my literary rock. You know, if you moved to the moon, I'd follow you there. Thank you for everything. Onward!
- Lynda Mullaly Hunt—whose talent is surpassed only by her generosity. Lynda, you are an inspiration to me in every way. This book simply would not exist without you.

Thank you to everyone who read early versions of *Ruby* and gave me encouraging feedback that made for a stronger story:

- Rachel Galligan, Ellie Galligan, Margaret Morrison, Maureen McInerney, Grace McInerney, Maryann Bastian, Nwal Sara, Anita Overgaard, Ann Morency, Kate Lynch, Mary Pierce, Sarah Albee, Lisa Rosenman, Beverly McRory, Thomas Ferruolo, Mary Ferruolo, Sue Ferruolo, Sophia Ferruolo, Andrew Ferruolo, Kimi Moretti, Les Moretti, Bryce Moretti, Trevor Moretti, Karen Zulick, and Olivia Zulick.
- Special thanks to Nora Brown for naming her goldfish Bob Van Doodle.

Thank you to the following friends who were willing to answer my endless questions in order to make this fictional story tell the truth:

- Dr. Suleiman and Lona Zalatimo, Sara Metz, Nour Shraiki, Huda Shraiki, Mahmood Mahmood, Bahaa Al-Tamimi, Maryam Kazadi, Drisyle Kazadi, Consolata Ndayishimiye, and Hilla Nasruddin. Thank you for sharing your unique experiences and expertise.

- Kathryn Fitzgerald and her students at Windermere School in Ellington, Connecticut, who made me feel like a real author before I was one. Thank you for your expert feedback on all things "sixth grade."

- The attorneys, social workers, investigators, and staff of public defender offices throughout the United States. Every day, public defenders bravely, passionately, and tirelessly lend their voices to those in greatest need. Thank you, especially, to the attorneys in Vermont and Connecticut whom I consulted about Dahlia's case. Any literary liberties taken with the law and court procedure rest solely with me.

- Ashley Makar and Ann O'Brien of IRIS—Integrated Refugee and Immigrant Services in New Haven, Connecticut (irisct.org). There is no better symbol of what our country stands for than the work you do.

Thank you for welcoming refugees into our country and me into your community.

It is easy for writers to become discouraged. The path to publication can be lonely, leaving plenty of opportunities for self-doubt to creep in. Thank you to the SCBWI Work-In-Progress, PEN New England Susan P. Bloom Children's Book Discovery, NESCBWI Ruth Landers Glass Scholarship, and New Voices in Children's Literature: Tassy Walden Award committees for honoring *Ruby in the Sky* with your recognitions. The important work you do inspires writers to keep going and improve their craft, and puts important books into the hands of the kids who need them. I am humbled by and grateful for your support.

As with any important journey, there are detours and obstacles along the way. I can't think about Ruby's struggles without remembering my own. Much of this book was written and revised as I recovered from chemotherapy to treat breast cancer, and again, later, as I recuperated from two surgeries to remove a rare sarcoma. Without the help, love, and support of so many friends and family, Ruby's voice would have been forever muted. Thank you to everyone who sent love in the form of prayers, cards, and visits. I want to especially thank Sue Ferruolo and Deb Zulick, who remained by my side through some less-than-fun hospital stays. A special thank-you to the amazing doctors and nurses at Smilow Cancer Hospital at Yale New Haven, especially Erin Wysong Hofstatter, MD; Gineesha Abraham, APRN; Anees Chagpar, MD; John W. Colberg, MD; and Elena Ratner, MD. It was under your care that Ruby found her voice and I regained mine.

Finally, no one is luckier than me to be part of the family I've been blessed with. A heart-shaped thank-you to:

- My husband, Paul—who introduced me to the wonder of snowshoe hikes at dawn—and to our amazing children, Andrew and Sophia. You are my sun and moon and stars.
- The Ferruolos, especially our patriarch, John A. Ferruolo—whose heart is larger than the moon itself and who, with Beverly McRory, shows us every day that family = love. I am so proud to be part of your clan.
- My parents, Barbara and John Zulick, and my siblings, Robert Zulick, Deborah Zulick, and Sarah Zulick Sardo. Our farm in Ashford, Connecticut, provided just the right soil to grow beautiful stories.

Thank you, Dad, for showing me the magic in hand-feeding chickadees. Even though you are no longer with us on Earth, I know I can always find you on the moon. Last, but most definitely not least: Mom, you are the glue that holds my world together. This book—this dream—is all because of you.